THE BUDDHIST [illegible]

Alex Torres

A Twisted Tail Tales book.
https://www.facebook.com/twistedtailuk/

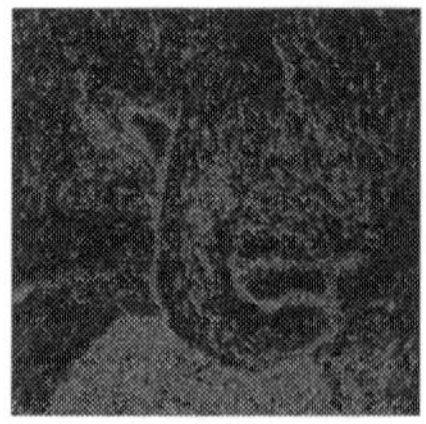

Cover designed by Alexandre Pinheiro-Torres
(Original images: (i) Multiwavelength Crab Nebula, Hubble Space Telescope Image May 2017, used under public domain rights granted by NASA and STScl; (ii) Pixabay image © Ulrike Mai, used under Pixabay CC0 licence)

First published July 2018 – Kindle eBook edition
This edition – August 2018

ISBN: 978-1-7178-1063-2

Also by Alex Torres:
The Fifties Child: A Social History Through the Songs of Barclay James Harvest (Desert Hearts, 2013)

One day, whilst I was struggling to finish writing my first book, a non-fiction social history based on the songs of a classic rock band, my wife said to me: "... but why don't you write a story about a rescued dog instead - that would be much better."

And so, my love, this is for you.

The Buddhist and the Bomber

I feel sorry for the bomber
Who all life and limb dishonours.
—JOHN LEES, from the song 'Summer Soldier', 1972

None of us is a monster, Chiku. We're all just trying to make the best of our singular natures.
—ALASTAIR REYNOLDS, from the novel 'On the Steel Breeze', 2013

Without my voice, and spirit, I am dust,
This is not what I want, but what I must.
—MIKE BARTLETT, from the play 'King Charles III', 2014

PROLOGUE

STATE POLICE HQ – THE CITY

The irony of the situation made the Inquisitor grin boyishly under his headgear. Looking up from his position on the floor, a few feet below the saracen, his victim looked like the crucified Christ silhouetted against the sunset. Caught in the ceiling spotlights behind the Extender Machine, the array of neural sensors attached to the saracen's head reminded the Inquisitor of Christ's crown of thorns. His arms were splayed wide by the tensioning wires, as in the crucifixion: only the outstretched legs betrayed the classic pose. But it was close enough.

How apposite, he thought.

No-one else would share this perspective. Other than the Inquisitor and the saracen, only the Tweaker was present, and he – or she – was consigned to the control console. Neither knew the other's identity: it was a necessary curse - or was it a blessing? – of this job. There would be no delight from sharing the image in the outside world either. A prime characteristic of these representatives of State was that they were loners – a thoroughly researched prerequisite of the job. In any case, this operation was covert beyond covert. The Inquisitor did not exist, nor did this Chamber.

Who needs company and the plaudits of others when you have a good imagination?

Store the memory, recall it at will, manifold joy.

Concentrate! he reminded himself.

The Controller had stressed the urgency of the situation. There was to be no opportunity for fun and games: this was work, pure and simple.

An absolute nuisance! They're so careful about protecting their secret that it takes them an age to extricate the victims from the normal spols. And then they deflect the pressure onto me! Typical! Don't they realise that one wrong move would terminate the saracen prematurely?

Sighing to himself, he raised his hand in a twirl. Taking his cue, the Tweaker adjusted the controls. The strops suspending the saracen from the Extender Machine tensioned. No scream emanated from the saracen's mouth: they were beyond that stage. But, turning his eyes slightly to the side, the Inquisitor was able to view the neural displays on the monitors within his headset. All indicators flipped red: excruciating pain.

Good. More left yet to use 'in extremis' if his willpower is stronger than anticipated. But he has already yielded useful information: there'll be no stoppering the rest now. Timing's the only factor at stake here.

"Tell me where and when, come on, it would be so very helpful."

Eyes bulging, staring. Not that the saracen could do anything else: Tortiebot had sown his eyelids back to his forehead so that he would never blink again. But there was no flicker of the lips either, no tell-tale oscillation on the displays.

Irritated, the Inquisitor flicked his hand angrily in an urgent gesture. The Tweaker understood and adjusted accordingly. The indicators leapt up into the purple. The Inquisitor thought that he detected a flicker of a grimace across the saracen's face.

Got him!

"Come on, where?"

"Th…lly…3.." A barely audible hiss, not even a whisper, but the Inquisitor was a good professional.

"Ah, the rally. At 3pm."

"..s"

The Inquisitor turned off sound projection and flipped channel.

"Controller?"

"Got it! The carrier? Urgent!" Etched with anxiety.

Switching back to in-chamber comms, the Inquisitor continued:

"Good, good, now we're getting somewhere. We're closer now, my friend. Just one more step and I can release you into that garden graced with flowing streams. So: who is the carrier?"

"..o."

The Inquisitor gestured to the Tweaker once again but received the dreaded buzzer alarm in response. No more tension was possible without termination.

On his fingerpad now, the Inquisitor quickly dialled up a pre-set instruction to Tortiebot. The 'bot approached the saracen, deploying a clamp tool above his buttocks. The tool's feelers reached down, gripped each cheek in turn and spread them wide.

"OK, so here's the deal," said the Inquisitor. "I'm going to ask you a question and you're going to give me a truthful answer. The probes in your head will warn me if you're lying. Now, if you don't answer truthfully, Tortiebot here will insert this probe up your anus. As you will find, you will not be able to clench it shut. Tortiebot will increase the probe's temperature – quickly or slowly, it depends – and you will cook from the inside out. A nice variation on burning at the stake – that's really very old fashioned. More painful though. Don't believe me? Just don't answer and you'll find out. Oh, and because Tortiebot is very clever, he can control the temperature so that we keep you roasting for weeks, basting – sorry, hydrating – you gently occasionally to ensure you don't leave us too soon."

Of course, the longevity claim was a wild exaggeration, but the gambit had worked well on previous occasions. Usually, one incandescence was sufficient to break the resistance. The Inquisitor continued unabated:

"However, should you wish to help us, I will simply give a signal to my digital friend and allow you to pass painlessly through the gate into that garden. Isn't that what you want? To wander through the garden graced with flowing streams? You could be there in seconds.

"So, who's the carrier?"

Nothing. No trace of movement, neither visual nor from the neural probes.

The Inquisitor touched a control. Tortiebot inserted the probe. All the signals shot up. The saracen gasped, impressing the Inquisitor with his resilience. He touched the controls again: Tortiebot withdrew the probe.

"You see? Good, isn't it? Be sure we can keep this up for weeks. We're clever. Any internal bleeding will just add to the agony. But we can also be congenial. I know where you want to go, the aim of your life's journey. And I have the key. I can open that gate. Let you walk through the gate. Into the garden. The garden graced with flowing streams.

"So, come on, who's the carrier? I promise, you'll be there immediately."

"…l….e.."

It wasn't quite enough. He indicated a reduction in tension to the Tweaker. The saracen would need his last breath to voice the answer.

"Sorry, didn't quite get that, one more time please and you'll be in the garden."

By the time that the Controller could act on the name, the saracen's spirit was already gambolling in the soft, aromatic grass of the garden graced with flowing streams.

♦ ♦ ♦

"People, we have the destination and the time. All droneyes and assdroids within a mile radius. Now! Scan for anomalous behaviour pending target ID."

No-one moved. Here, in the lightless RCR, all action was at a distance. All of the operatives, including the Controller, were strapped into their VR cubicles, whether operating droneyes or assdroids. Nevertheless, the tension was intense, transmitted palpably through the Controller's urgent, almost desperate, instructions.

"Come on, come on, someone must be seeing something unusual. Come on, guys, come on! We have very little time here! Find the carrier, guys, please, must be obvious!

"Hold! OK, got a name. Here. Month's bonus to whoever gets the visual first.

"Oh, come on! Who's not in the net these days? Some other way then. Come on, people, outside the box, remember? Come on!

"Lima Charlie, you got it! OK, people, we have visual. Here we go. Assdroids to atomisation level! Locate and lock-in! Now!"

"Controller, I have ID. Running onto the bridge, towards the centre."

"Assdroids, down target! Now!"

PART 1
BEGINNINGS

1 THE CITY

Can we say that there is something special about this city?

No.

Of course, it does have a lofty status to many of its inhabitants on account of it being their birthplace, their home, the place where they feel safe snuggled down in their nests. But, by any other reckoning, this is an ordinary city. You and I only have to raise our vantage point.

Yes, come up with me and look down below.

See?

Fairly ordinary, wouldn't you say? Even the impressive buildings, so tall and domineering when seen from the ground, and the imposing, portentous monuments, fade away into the muddle once you gain some perspective.

And look yonder, just over there. The neighbouring town: doesn't it look the same viewed from here? I'll lay you a wager that the city just over the horizon – there, see it now? - looks the same.

So, no, there's nothing special about this city.

Wait a moment!

Before we go back, linger awhile and listen to the silence up here. Let it seep into and become a part of you, feel it enter your every limb, your sinews, your lungs, your cells, your blood.

Drink!

Drink your fill of the silence.

Feel the waves of the wind rushing past the hairs on your skin, waggling them in a crazy dance; feel it cool your body and watch the heat eddy away as the atoms roar past.

Go!

Go with that flow, surf your swirling energy on its mazy journey around the globe, into the oceans and out again.

Be amazed!

2 THE STREET

The street itself had been marooned for some years now, abandoned by the dusty ways of time. Progress had promoted its parallel sisters to the status of vital arteries that fed the centre with its daily lifeblood of workers and shoppers. Money making, money spending, round and round the body of the city they flowed, pumped up with lust for more.

The unleashing of greed.

The relentless pursuit of more.

More!

The workers' and shoppers' indefatigable vibrancy helped the city to grow, its health evident by the tall buildings that phoenixed from the rubble of last century's war. But, despite the edifices' shrouding impact on the skyline, the spying eyes of St. Peter's soaring steeple still tendrilled their perpetual gaze over the city.

Vigilance was a constant necessity in the battle to save souls!

Why, just there, barely two blocks away, St. Peter could stare straight into the eyes of that traitor, St. David, pandering to the Protestants. And, if he concentrated, he could detect a decaying Baptist breath, carried from farther away on the troublesome wind, tickling at the stones on the nape of his steeple.

Troublesome wind, yes. It was the harbinger of threats far greater than that posed by Protestants and Baptists. The scent spectrum on the breeze warned him of the proximity of a dagerpode. Worse, if he inhaled deeply it would cause him to shrivel involuntarily as slugs of acrid air seared the gullet of his sanctuary - a kroda! It must be hidden there, a couple of streets away, towards the castle and the park, camouflaged by the houses.

A kroda!

Was this why I sent holy men to fight in the Crusades? Their souls will burn with incense.

St. Peter's influence had once been absolute, shaping the minds of kings. He had been the effective ruler of the civilized world. The saracen had risen to challenge his might, conquering all before them. But his minions had fought them back, and had then taken to the seas, brave explorers all, in the desire to find new souls to convert to God's truth. Millions of new worshippers would glorify His name. And the glory would reflect back on St. Peter.

Or was it the desire for new knowledge to sate their minds that drove them onwards? Or the lust for imagined riches? The craving for worldly dominance?

Oh, how age weighs down upon my stones! Too old to remember.

The explorer heroes had been successful, to the extent that even St. Peter became infatuated with the accumulation of treasure from the conquest of heathen lands. But, despite his great power, St. Peter had to rely on Man, incarcerated as he was in holy stones. And the mind of Man, warped by greed, had become addled with schemes of supremacy. Man schemed against St. Peter, founding his own churches with rules that better suited his ambition. St. Peter's domination waned. As Man's science inflated his ego, he began to create more and more gods and churches in his own image. A new church for every new situation: that was the approach. The pantheon expanded with shiny items of mass worship.

Wealth.

Media.

Celebrity.

St. Peter was left with virtually no leverage in the modern world. True, a few worshippers still trundled through his portico, mostly more through fear than devotion, but he was an emasculated force compared to the shaper of destinies of centuries past.

And so St. Peter scanned the city, his prying constant, anxious for any signs of further threats to the last vestiges of his authority. At any moment he might spot some Jehovah's Witnesses: they were easy, for they always dressed immaculately and hunted in pairs. Or he might see a father and his sons walking to dagerpode, their skull-capped deportment darting its alienation deep into the heart of his nave. Much worse would be sightings of ambulating black-garbed monoliths, all darkness and secrecy personified.

Any such apparitions would always pain him, but what could he do? For all the splendour of his steeple and the magnificence of his massive bells, he was now dependent on the puny Father Cuthbert. The priest's youthfulness and good looks might have lured a flush of dry spinsters to his altar but his ability to influence events was dampened by the daily chores of parish visits. His days were devoured by an endless procession of tea and cake with dowdy dowagers as the city's population aged gracelessly, or with in-fighting committees for this, that or the other trifling issue. Oh, how St. Peter longed for the good old days when he reigned supreme; when the words emanating from his pulpit were sufficient to make people quake.

Those were the days that he yearned for. His bells rang loud and often, asserting his might. News, events, celebrations, warnings, calls to action. The reverberation would be heard for miles, reaching all of the surrounding villages. And no-one dared complain about the noise.

No, in those days Ministers of Government would come to him on their knees, sometimes daily, and beg him to control the people, make them understand how to comply with the law. And their offerings were bountiful. Now, the Ministers never came, for they were too busy flattering the Celebrities that carried their pathetic messages to the populace.

Withered and distraught, he fretted, enduringly clinging on to the hope that, if he was watchful, he might one day find an opportunity to recover his former glory. That whisker of hope was all that remained to sustain St. Peter.

And so he watched, constantly. And he worried, constantly.

The street concerned him. Not that there was much to see.

Or is there? I can sense something, feel it in my stones. There must be...

It was treeless, the elms long dead. Blotches of weed-ridden earth marked the place where they had once stood, ostentatiously displaying their mighty reach, before the arterial avenues revitalised the city and condemned the street to decay. Dust swirled in from all around and, in a clash of whirlwinds, settled conspiratorially, as if part of a grand design to entomb the street. The dingy garage selling discounted servicing was the only business, advertising its prowess by displaying the skeletons of rusty cars in its courtyard. St. Peter had never actually seen any clients arriving or leaving and so had long ago consigned the dilapidated mess within his own mind as a tax dodge.

Rows of tired and featureless terraced houses stared unblinking at each other across the street, standing with military stillness, as if waiting to salute the inspecting dignitaries that never came. Virtually nothing moved by day, the residents either ensconced in their nests or busying themselves eking out a living, keeping the city, not the street, alive. Here, in this street, lived the worker ants, the termites, the busy bees that firmed up the city's vital structures. Teachers, refuse collectors, nurses, bus drivers, firemen, social workers: the great unseen and unglamorous without which the edifice would collapse. The street acted like a magnet for students too, attracted by lower rents and unfussy neighbours. St. Peter could hear their music filtering through his pews in the early hours of the morning: it caused the dust in his pores to vibrate in unison, irritating his stones, discomforting him.

St. Peter would often recall street scenes from yesteryear with fondness. Women and children happily busying and playing during daylight. Now the mothers had deserted the street, needing to work to keep the nest alive, or striving for their own wealth, or perhaps just driven by peer pressure. Their children would be educated in the jungle world of kindergarten and nursery, agonising in others' care.

The night was a particular worry to him. The city council had long ago decided that, in order to save its ratepayers money, backwater streets would not have lighting after midnight. The only illumination St. Peter had for his ritualistic spying was diffracted through slits in drawn curtains or, occasionally, from the dim glow of city lights reflected off an oppressive cloud base. Neither was entirely sufficient for an old man of God such as he. But St. Peter hadn't survived for over two thousand years by relying on a single sense. After all, he did have God on his side. And so he concentrated, focusing his steeple, enhancing its capabilities.

And, in so doing, he monitored the street and beyond.

♦ ♦ ♦

Cloud blankets the city. No moonlight filters through its thick mass. St. Peter can see virtually nothing. The street appears to be empty. Sharp wind vortices, aspiring to be baby tornadoes, whip up the dust in dark corners. Here and there mice, ousted by their own burgeoning families, dart over walls or fences in search of a new abode, hiding in the shadows, scuttling fearfully. Wheelie bins - the houses' smelly feet – stand very still, festering malodorously. Weathered posters, advertising concerts from bygone years, billow in the wind like rastafarian locks. Lampposts sway gently, grey and redundant.

But wait.

Pay attention, St. Peter!

Take a closer look and listen. Especially listen. Hone in your bells. Tune in to their subtle oscillation. Can you hear? That rattling sound, interspersed with scraping. Intermittent and faint, yet surely there, like the heartbeat of a dying leper.

Where? Must find it, must find it.

Listen, listen hard St. Peter, for if you stop listening then it may vanish altogether, like the life slowly ebbing out of your chalice.

3 THE RESCUE

How did I come to be trapped there? I must have been asleep when it happened because I've never been able to recall that part of my memory. In fact, I have no memory of a time before that. Did I even exist at all then?

♦ ♦ ♦

I become conscious - startled, with a thump - and feel sensations of falling, slipping, being continuously bumped on my back and sides, but I quickly come to a halt.

It is dark.

Are my eyes open?

I can see nothing. I must be awake because I can smell a pungent odour that is making me retch.

I feel wedged, blocked in all around, pressure on every part of my body. I'm not certain that I'm upright but I try to move, gently at first. There's no headway to be made to the left or the right. My nose keeps bumping into objects that yield slightly but firmly resist any movement when I push harder. Sounds are muffled too, dull and low, equally unable to escape this prison.

If I have fallen, then I should try and climb. I have to escape from this cornucopia of stench.

I wriggle hard and twist, managing to make some headway in what I sense is up, although, to be honest, I'm a little confused. I pause, waiting to see if the falling sensation resumes. It doesn't. I scraggle a bit more and my head works loose of pressure, as if there is nothing more above.

Hope rekindled!

I paddle strenuously and am rewarded: I feel something under me that can only be described as squidgy ground. Excited, I speed up my movement but bump my nose again, only this time into something much harder and more unyielding. Ouch! Turning quickly and moving to the left produces the same result: ouch!

Stop.

Think.

Where am I?

The air is foul with putrid fumes and the pong makes me retch again. I recompose myself, turn around, step forward. Ouch! Try the right: ow! Go diagonal but I tumble again, bumping as before and become wedged. I feel the pressure all over, pushing on the top of my head, at my eyes, my whole face, making it difficult to draw breath.

Frantic now, flailing wildly, I move slightly but then feel the same hard wall as I hammer and scrape at an unyielding surface. I paddle harder again, trying to instil some upward motion. It's no good. All I achieve is inhaling more of the foul smell and now, panic rising, I vomit the contents of my stomach. There's nowhere for the gunk to go. I am coated in acrid bile. The smell is almost unbearable but I cannot escape it. I am too frightened to breathe for fear of sucking more in, so begin taking shallow breaths and holding the air in for as long as I can tolerate it. The struggle is warping my mind.

Stop.

Think.

Ignore the smell, put it out of mind.

Concentrate.

There must be a way out of this place. I have to get my head up above these soft, bumpy barriers, back to that type of plain where I was before. Replicate my previous moves, go from there, build up knowledge of this unfathomable maze.

So: more effort, and I find myself once again feeling as though I am level, standing shakily on this slightly soft, plastic-feeling terrain. But when I try to move off again, the same hard structure prevents me from progressing more than a few paces in any direction. With every turn there is a barrier and the unrelenting dark. Just blackness. No contrast, no light, not even a retinal flicker. Only the stinking smells of decay.

Exhaustion sweeps through me, muffles my anxiety. I try to vocalize my despair but the sound is feeble, constrained within my prison. I flop and rest, luxuriating in stillness. Whether from frustration or the fetid air, the panic eases to a feeling of resigned acceptance. Trapped as I am, I close my eyes – were they ever open? – and feel sleep coming on.

Must fight sleep!

Must stay awake, watchful for an opportunity to escape. Is that a forlorn hope?

I have no sense of time passing, no way of measuring it except through the slowing musings of my mind. The fatigue is overwhelming and the temptation to doze again is irresistible. I try to control the depth of unconsciousness by monitoring the pressure on my body. When I feel my concentration slip, the beginning of deep sleep, I muster my willpower and try some more scrabbling. As a result, I shift and move around this dark dungeon. I find the occasional aromatic morsel amongst the detritus. I do a lick test before eating. But there's not enough food.

Hunger berates my stomach.

Thirst tightens my throat.

I try and focus my mind elsewhere but the pain is not totally dulled.

Try to stay awake, remain alert.

It has become very hot. The air, which has been musty from the beginning of my ordeal, now has rancid urine in its bouquet. I can no longer sustain prolonged attempts at rushing, bashing or bouncing. My efforts to escape have virtually ceased.

I am exhausted, ready to accept defeat, ready to accept fate and surrender completely to peaceful sleep.

Sleep, welcoming sleep.

Suddenly, almost at the end of hope, I feel an astounding sensation envelop my body, as if each cell has been individually zapped with a boost of life energy, each vibrating in unison with its neighbour, making my whole being resonate with vigour.

This cannot be!

I start to jump wildly, infused with this irresistible energy, yipping with my excitement. I keep missing my footing as I land, falling repeatedly, but the force of will that is now driving me on overwhelms all setbacks. I leap upwards again and again, bashing into the hard obstacles, yielding the soft.

This cannot be!

I will be free!

Yelp. Yelp. Yelp!

Shock!

I feel a massive thwack on my muzzle coincident with a sound like thunder and tumble backwards wincing with pain. Almost simultaneously there's another humongous crashing sound and I get another painful bash to the back of the head as I'm sent cartwheeling. Then – heavenly! - I feel a rush of wind on my face as I roll and skid along the ground. When I come to a standstill, spread-eagled, the taste of street dust is on my tongue.

I'm outside!

My muzzle is being licked now. I can feel the moistness and light pressure of a caring tongue slowly cleaning me, sprucing me up after my ordeal. It feels glorious after my rank prison and I just lie there, enjoying the fuss and the cool night air. Yes, I'm sure it is night-time. The only dim illumination comes from the orange hue off the low clouds. Regardless, I wouldn't be able to see much of the bitch that is washing me fastidiously because she is too close to my face. Her aroma and presence are unmistakable so I know that she is definitely a bitch. My nose is still being licked, then my lips and my ears receive the same thorough treatment. She stops momentarily, presumably to inspect the effectiveness of her efforts, then restarts on my body, which is gunky from my struggle in the wheelie bin.

A wheelie bin?

How did I possibly get in there? I can see its silhouette against the pavement, rubbish strewn all over the road, now that my saviour has moved on from my head.

4 THE RESCUE

Isn't it peculiar how some specific memories stay fresh, regardless of the passage of time, whereas countless others perish, never again to live through the electricity of thought? What is it that defines those special moments, that makes them live on? This account is based purely on that subset. Would others give the lie to this tale, were they to recall the same times? What follows are my own recollections and I present them to you in good faith.

♦ ♦ ♦

We lived near the top of a hill in one of the smarter areas of the city. Our house, however, was small, part of a terrace in a cul-de-sac that ran flat along the gradient. From the upstairs window there was an expansive view across to the west, the sea sometimes imagined visible in the distance, the large hospital dominating the skyline.

Down the hill itself, set either side of the main drive, were the bigger houses, detached and semi-detached, sporting bigger, newer cars and wealthier residents. In truth, I didn't know much about the people who lived in these houses. Occasionally, when I was very young, I'd been invited in to play with other boys who lived there and I'd always been overawed by the opulence of the soft carpets and cushioned sofas. My parents hadn't approved of these visits and had restricted them by forcing me to stay at home. There would always be some ludicrous excuse. You can't go out because of this; you can't go out because of that. It didn't have to make sense: this was total control. Also, because I'd been sent to a Catholic denominational school, I saw these boys less often and our friendship faded naturally as I developed into puberty.

I was no longer welcome in these houses. Until, that is, the day of the accident.

If I concentrate, I can still feel the touch of the wind billowing through my hair. I was being bolder than usual and the feeling was enthralling as I gathered speed skating down the hill. Pushing at the surface, I made myself go even faster, then settled, knees flexed. But my daring had outreached my ability. The increasing rush of ground alarmed me, as did the heightened noise and vibration. Worse still, I suddenly realized that I didn't know how to slow down on the steep slope. How was I going to make the sharp turn at the bottom without falling?

I needn't have worried. I never reached the bottom. One of my skates must have hit a stone on the road. I couldn't have been in the air for long but the sensation of disconnectedness as I hurtled headlong has stayed with me forever. The impact was harsh. Instinctively, I managed to soften the fall with my hands and arms but my face still hit the ground. I heard a loud clunk in my brain and felt a burning sensation from my chin, lips and nose. Simultaneous searing pain from my knees announced that their fleshy covering had been ripped by the gravelly surface. I hadn't even had the protection of trousers: serve me right for wearing shorts.

I lay there without moving, stunned and winded, the pain shrouding all thought, for how long I do not know, until I was induced to look up by a man's gentle voice.

"Son, are you alright?"

I'd known that there was a black man living in a house down on the hill. I'd seen him from afar but had never met him before. His voice was soothing and gentle, his large brown eyes oozing sympathy.

"My, you're in a state. Here, let me help you. Can you stand?"

"No," I blubbed, sobbing. "Don't think so."

"Come on, let's carry you in and clean you up. I think you're going to be absolutely fine. Let's just take this off first."

One of the skates had been ripped off in the fall but the other was clinging on. The black man undid the strap and removed it. Then he hooked one arm - skates dangling from his hand - under my knees and the other round my shoulders, lifting me up seemingly without effort. He smiled kindly and his words relieved my aches and woes:

"Don't worry, sshhh, you're OK. We'll soon have you sorted."

It transpired that I'd fallen right outside his house. He had left the front door ajar and lent on it with his back, swivelling me in. The hallway was wide - much wider than that of our own terraced house just up the hill - and its light décor reflected the sunlight streaming in through the half-glazed door. Its effect was calming, cocooning, and I relaxed in the man's care.

"Mimi! Mimi, come and help please," he called.

A faint reply came from an upstairs bedroom: "Yes, dad."

The man carried me into the kitchen. It was huge: there was even space for a small dining table. He pulled one of the chairs out and lowered me carefully onto it.

"Right, then, brave soldier, let's clean you up, shall we? Mimi, fetch me the first aid kit please whilst I wash this young man's wounds."

Mimi had barely entered the kitchen before she scampered off again.

That brief appearance in the doorway remains with me still, the image etched in brilliant colours in every corner of my mind, the feeling of wonder seared into every cell of my body. I recognised her from school. She was in a different class and I had only previously seen her from afar. I had thought she was pretty but had been too busy with playground games to focus. She had never looked as enchanting as this at school.

Framed in the doorway for that split second, aglow in a beam of miraculous light, she seemed like an angel descended from heaven. Her straight black hair hung loose down to her shoulders; evocative brown eyes, a cute turned up nose and an inviting mouth set her face aflame. Mimi was a mulatta, her skin a spotless hazel hue, glistening with life. She was dazzling!

"What's your name, young man?"

"Michael, sir." Shaken by Mimi's appearance, I could barely mutter the usual half-lie.

"Michael. Welcome to our humble house. I'm Tennyson. That was quite a tumble you took out there, but it seems as if you've escaped relatively lightly. This is mainly just a bit of grit. Surface wounds and scratches. I'll wash all this muck off with some clean water, then we'll apply some lotion and you'll be fit again in no time."

Mr. Tennyson poured some water from the kettle into a bowl and fetched a pile of paper napkins.

"Here, roll this napkin up, then you can bite into it if it stings when I start to wash your cuts."

I took it but there was no way I'd be squealing in front of Mimi.

"Thanks, Mimi," he said when she returned with the first aid box. "Mimi, do you know Michael? Say hello."

Mimi sat at the opposite end of the table. She looked serene, peaceful, in unity with the air itself. She smiled, the radiance warming my skin like sunlight in winter. "He goes to my school. Hello."

"Ah, so you're friends."

"Well, not exactly, but I've seen him walking to school."

Transfixed, I couldn't speak. My heart raced, urging me to seize the moment. I couldn't. I was dumb.

"Pass me a towel please, Mimi, then the iodine tincture." Mr. Tennyson cleaned my wounds with the boiled water, then gently dabbed them dry. He oozed confidence and his calm demeanour seemed to dampen the pain.

"OK, Michael, that's all the gunk out of your cuts. I'll apply some of this stuff now – magic healing! – but it might just sting a bit. Oh, and it'll leave a stain for a few days. OK?"

"Yes, sir."

"Bite away."

I tried to brave it out of course, because Mimi was watching me intently, but I had to have one bite to avoid crying out when Mr. Tennyson worked on my chin.

"There, all done. Wounds all cleaned and disinfected. Would you like a drink of water?"

"No, thank you, sir, I'm alright."

"Alright, then, perhaps we'd better take you back home. Do you live on the Drive?"

"No, sir, I'm up at the Close, number 5." The Close. Terraced house. Patchwork garden. Small kitchen. Threadbare carpets. Trashy second-hand car. I felt inferior.

"OK, then, let's see how well you can walk. Here, first, come into the downstairs bathroom and look in the mirror. The tincture spots look a little comical. What do you think, Mimi?"

"He looks funny." Her eyes lived that truth, sparkled light that dazzled me. I tried to return the smile but my face hurt, so lowered my eyes.

"Yes, well, the wounds will heal quickly and not leave a scar, so it's worth it for a few days. We'd better tell your mum what you've been up to, eh? Come on, I'll come and explain these blotches."

"Bye, Michael."

I melted.

"Bye."

My knees stung from the fall so we walked slowly up the hill to the Close. Mr. Tennyson carried my roller skates and held a friendly arm around my shoulders as I half leaned into him for support. I distinctly remember how content I felt, despite my wounds and the pain. Mr. Tennyson's quiet, peaceful confidence had calmed me and I felt happy.

That idyll was shattered as soon as my mum came to the door. Judging from her vitriolic reaction, you'd have believed that Mr. Tennyson had punched her.

"Oh, Jesus! What have you done? What's happened to your face?" she screamed.

"Madam, young Michael here fell off his roller skates right outside my house. He was badly shaken. His face, knees, hands were badly cut up. I helped him up and cleaned him up a little. This here's iodine tincture; it'll heal his wounds in no time. He'll be just fine."

"You leave my son alone, mister. Don't you go messing with my son. What have you done to him? Get on out of here. Scram!"

"But, madam, your son was hurt, I just helped him."

"Don't you go messing with my son! Out of here. Go on! Get in here, boy."

She dragged me into the hallway, slammed the door in Mr. Tennyson's face and slapped me across the head.

"Get to your bedroom. Now!"

Stunned, I ran upstairs to my room, gammy knees stinging ferociously with the bending. I threw myself face down on the bed and wept, overwhelmed with emotions, brain ascramble. It must have been some minutes later when my mum finally came up to see me. She had barely calmed down.

"I do not want you associating with that man. Ever. He should have brought you straight back here, not messed around with you like this – just look at you."

"I was hurt, mum. He helped me."

"He did no such thing. Let me see those wounds."

She yanked my face towards her and inspected my chin closely, then snatched my hands palm upwards, examined them and finally roughly gripped my calves to look at my knees.

"They're clean."

She was flushed, clearly irritated, disappointed even. Mr. Tennyson had done a good job.

"Wait 'til your father hears about this!"

Storming out, she hammered the door shut. The walls shook.

Father. She meant the word to be a threat and it had its intended effect. Father. My overbearing, disciplinarian, academic of a father, forced to turn bus driver in a foreign country after his semi-forced exile from totalitarianism. He had never felt at home here, the city in which I had to make my day-to-day life, running the gamut of the vicious jungle of the school battlefield. He always wanted to be away, yearned to go back 'home'. But this was home for me. I had been brought over as a young child and now had little or no fondness for that dusty land. The gulf between us was distant and unbridgeable. His and mum's very presence, very existence in this world jeopardized my integration into my new home. Their heavy accents were enough to betray my own unsavoury origins to any friends that might come round to play. How could I integrate? How could I pretend to be normal like everyone else with them around? How could I live the lie? Michael, not Miguel?

My parents held my life in their hands, strangling its spirit.

Mum's warning had not been idle. My father returned home punctually, expecting his dinner to be served at the appointed time. I kissed his cheeks in a mock welcome: to ignore the ritual was an insult with exceptionally unpleasant consequences. He ignored my facial disfigurement while mum updated him with the day's developments.

Then, when he finally spoke, assuredly erudite, the bile in his voice burned my body, as if I'd taken a long draught of potent acid that instantly infiltrated to every cell. I curdled at his words:

"You will never associate with that black man again. Dirty filth!"

My faith in my parents was shattered. Life would never be the same again.

◆ ◆ ◆

Marooned in my bedroom after a silent family dinner noisy with aggressive stares, I lay on the bed and succumbed to the maelstrom of my mind. Thoughts spun viciously like the swirling galaxies that I imagined seeing straight out of the window.

I allowed my gaze to fly light years away.

Just there, look.

The imagined vista took my breath away. I stumbled off the bed and stepped to the window, resting my forehead against the cool glass. I breathed in the night air, following the direction of my breath to focus in and out of the cityscape:

…

in

…

out

…

city

…

galaxy

…

in

…

The mental turmoil subsided. Sublimating out of its chaos emerged some fundamental ideas that would ingrain themselves in my soul like rocks in a cooling lava flow.

Ironic.

Unjust.

Ironic, yes. Here we were, our family virtually outcasts in this city, our foreignness all too evident and easy fodder for the vitriol of natives, yet still prepared to feel prejudice against others in the same position.

And how unjust. Mr. Tennyson had been kind, invited me into his home, bathed my wounds. He had shown friendship and compassion. Were my mother's insults just reward? No, not once in all its pirouettes did my mind consider it just.

Her behaviour and my father's subsequent condemnation of Mr. Tennyson were fundamentally not right.

And yet…

Slicing through these travesties like the beauty of snowflakes reflecting moonlight, abating the terror of night, was Mimi's transcendent appearance. She invaded my mind again and again, so that when I finally drifted into sleep, she was as ingrained in my psyche as the injustice of bigoted judgement.

5 NEW FRIENDS

I was enjoying my bath. As the bitch's tongue wiped away the last traces of filth, I was rocked gently from side to side. I rolled over and lay on my back, pawed the air playfully and was rewarded with a tummy tickling. I giggled and squirmed with delight. The bitch clearly took this as an indication that I was feeling better and stopped the obsessive washing, moving off to sit close by, eyeing me intently.

I stood and teased her but my cute bumwiggle and pleading airpawing had no effect: she continued to sit serenely, as if all the time in the world and more was hers. Slightly disconcerted, I sat and tried to return her stare. She had short, dirty brown hair with black flecking. Her ears were large, well out of proportion with her head, and upright, gently twitching this way and that, constantly on the move, monitoring.

Sensing no danger, I waddled over and sniffed her. She was very earthy, but nicely so. I licked her flank and tasted fine specks of dust, sweet and flavoursome like the leftovers of a feast. Now that I was up close I could feel her bodily warmth and I snuggled up for comfort. She stood and I wriggled under her to continue exploring. Her nipples were cold and hard when I suckled them: no milk there. I moved on to smell her vent: her digestion was good. Her buttocks were clean, her tail fluffy and the hairs loose and soft. All very nice. Walking round, I savoured the aroma around her muzzle and licked her chops: she'd eaten recently. My tummy rumbled at this prompt of food and I tasted her jowl again. She returned the licking and checked my own vent. I took affront because she had only just finished cleaning me and so I twisted away and faced her. Unperturbed by my daring, she flicked me firmly on the muzzle once more, then turned and trotted off imperiously.

Pausing a few yards off, she checked to see if I was following and, encouraged by a gentle wag of her tail and a magnetism I couldn't resist, I did so, needing to run as hard as I could to keep up.

There was no-one else around on the street as we trotted along. The bitch seemed to know exactly where she was going. She kept a steady, confident pace and gave me no time to stop and carefully sniff my surroundings. The light intensified subtly, enough for me to see that we were approaching a huge building with a tall tower. My saviour turned off the street and walked up the broad stone steps that led to its entrance porch. I followed, noticing a disconcerting murmur emanating from the building itself. It was even discernible above the muffled roar of the traffic in the distance. I hesitated and paused briefly but the bitch didn't seem bothered by the menacing sound and, persuaded by her carefree advance, I continued on up the steps. Her earthy aroma dominated the atmosphere within the porch itself.

"Hello, Mullet. Who's that you've got with you? What a cute puppy."

I hadn't spotted the man until he'd spoken. He was sheltering from the wind, lying on a cardboard mattress, huddled up against the wall. It wasn't a pretty sight. His great bushy beard was splayed out over a mangy, dusty overcoat. It was obvious that the earthy smell was principally exuding from him: it welled up and concentrated in parts of the porch, covering him like a bubble blanket. I wouldn't say that it was particularly unpleasant, certainly not to me, but it was distinctive and strong, pervading the space and those around him. Its very organic texture soothed me like a lullaby, making me feel as though I belonged here, with these beings. I knew instinctively that they would be my home.

Mullet, for that must be my saviour's name, was clearly pleased to see the man and licked his face and beard enthusiastically in greeting. He grabbed her ears and muzzle lovingly in return, before giving her a brief but affectionate lick.

"Where did you get this little fella from then, hey?"

The man's voice was warm, his tone friendly. Mullet's earthy aroma was derived from him. It was obvious that there was a strong bond between them. I liked the man. He swept me off my paws and held me up, twirling me round, then snuggled me up to his chest and kissed my head tenderly. Mullet came up, pushed in and licked his mouth, pawing at his shoulder.

"Are you hungry, little fella? Let's see what we've got then, shall we?"

He retrieved a folded plastic bag from within the recesses of his overcoat. As soon as he opened it a delicious perfume pierced the earthiness of the air and infiltrated my nostrils. I stumbled forward to taste whatever delicacy might be producing such an enticing scent, but Mullet growled me back and I fell off the man's chest. I feigned calmness by giving myself a nonchalant lick on the rump and then sat alongside her, shifting impatiently on my vent.

"Now then, little fella, do you like pizza? Here, try this little bit."

He held it out for me to take. Mullet watched intently but didn't object and so I reached out and took it.

Wow!

There was an explosion of taste and sensation on my tongue: part of it was crunchy, part soft and the flavour was intense, dancing circles in my mouth as I absorbed the morsel. I squirmed forward on my vent but Mullet had the next piece; then the man helped himself to a couple of mouthfuls – unfairly large they seemed to me – before I was given another scrumptious scrap.

"There, have some of this."

He had delved into his overcoat again and produced some bread. It was dry and tasteless compared to the pizza but I was hungry and ate it up; Mullet too.

"There's a good boy."

The friendly man lifted me up in the air again and twizzled me round joyfully before placing me gently by a bowl of water that was tucked away in a corner of the porch.

"That's it. Cor, you were thirsty weren't you?" He paused briefly whilst I lapped greedily. "What are we going to call you then? Eh, little fella?"

I stopped drinking, startled as the massive door that led into the building creaked loudly, then opened slowly. A tall man walked out onto the porch, clutching a bulky paper bag to his chest.

"Good evening, Jake," he said.

"Good evening, Father. You're up late."

The man was dressed in simple, unadorned black clothes, the only colour being a white collar round his neck.

"Struggling to sleep, things on my mind. Look, I've brought you some scones that were left over from the parish sub-committee meeting this afternoon. You and Mullet may appreciate them. Oh! I see you have a new dog?"

The man handed the bag over to Jake, who opened it gingerly and, holding it up to his face, breathed in its aroma, sighing with satisfaction.

"Mullet brought him just now," said Jake. "Cute, eh? Not sure where he's from. He's not wearing a collar. Judging by the state of him he was abandoned. I can see Mullet's had a go at cleaning him up but she's left a few bits. And he's famished."

"Will you be keeping him, Jake? Will he not be too much trouble, with Mullet and all?"

Jake started breaking up the scones with his fingers, taking a piece for himself first, then placing one in Mullet's mouth, then mine in turn.

Delish.

I could barely contain my bumwiggle in anticipation of the next morsel.

"I can hardly kick him away, Father. I guess I'll wait and see what happens."

We carried on working our way through the scones, munching happily, Father taking a fair share. When the scones were finished and he'd swallowed his last piece, he continued:

"Well, I know I've always welcomed you here, Jake, but I need to have a word. You see, some of the ladies in the parish have mentioned that they find you intimidating if they come to the church for a quiet prayer on their own in the late evening or at night."

"I never say anything to them, Father, I just sit here quietly with Mullet, resting."

Jake scrunched up the scones bag, stashing it somewhere deep inside his overcoat. I could contain myself no longer and scrabbled up his chest, trying to nose my way into the overcoat after any last remaining crumbs. Jake flicked my muzzle away and placed me back down next to Mullet. Anyway, my trick worked because he had deviously hidden a whole scone in that cavernous space, which he kindly broke up with his fingers, then gently popped small, gorgeous pieces into our mouths.

"No, I know," said Father. "They're slightly sensitive, but perhaps whilst we're enjoying this good spell of weather you could find some other dry places to sleep, at least until Lent is over and the ladies return to their normal ways. You've not tried the shelter again, then?"

"No, Father. They didn't welcome Mullet and I found some of the other residents quite intimidating myself. I prefer my own company, and that of Mullet of course. I can stay out of trouble better that way. Plus, I might have this little fella to look after now, as well as Mullet."

"But it's not helping you find a job, is it Jake?"

"Oh, be realistic, Father, you know that those days are over for me. No-one would take me on after what happened last time even if I could find somewhere to live. And what would I do with these dogs? Mullet's been with me too long now for us to part and this little fella's only a pup. I'll do the odd casual stuff in the season out on the farms but there's no going back to mainstream employment for me."

It was Father's turn to lift me up gently. He started cuddling me, smoothing my ears between his fingers and scratching my head lightly.

"Well, I guess you're right: it would be difficult after what happened. I don't know, Jake. It seems as if there's no way out of this rut that you're in."

"I'm quite happy as I am, Father. I'm not like some of the others who've fallen into this life and are dejected and desperate for a way to improve their lot. I chose this way. I had my eyes open when I did what I did. I understood the consequences and I've always been happy to accept them. Mullet and I, we get along, we have a strong bond. She gives me a lot, you know? Some people, like you, are kind, and that always helps. We get enough to eat, one way or another." Jake paused briefly, as if churning thoughts in his mind, before continuing. "Though it did help last winter when you let us sleep inside the church during the worst of the cold."

"Yes, well, just don't get caught. The Bishop will have me burnt at the stake. He's not that keen on me, thinks I'm too radical, too full of ideas. Any excuse and he'll have me out of here."

"Ideas, eh? Dangerous for a priest. But you've not been here very long, Father."

Father plonked me down on Jake's stomach, then reached into his pocket. He had yet another scone ensconced in there. How come we hadn't sniffed it out? He nibbled at it thoughtfully for a moment, then placed a morsel in my mouth before resuming the luscious ear massage.

"Some of what I've been saying in my sermons has got back to him. You know, about the war in the south and the need to seek better integration with other communities and faiths in our own city. He doesn't go in for all that; wants his priests to focus on tradition, ceremony and ritual. Accent old Christian values. That's how he thinks we'll win our full congregations back."

"And when did compassion cease to be an old Christian value?"

"Well, the Bishop thinks we need to save souls for the Catholic Church. You know: here we are at St. Peter's, so 'go and be a fisher of men'. For us. He's not really hot on ecumenical ideas or syncretism. Anyway, neither are a couple of my own parishioners it seems, because it's they who've written to him with complaints."

"No! There's gratitude, eh? So what'll you do, Father?"

"I'm not sure. Pray. See where my soul leads. But I don't think that I can do too much more without overstepping the mark."

"Surely, Father, you have to be true to yourself. You have to follow your soul."

"Yes, Jake, but what if I'm moved on? What then? One of the Bishop's cronies in here? I might have to compromise. Say and do just enough to point people in the right direction without overcommitting myself."

"A tricky business, Father."

"Yes, Jake, sure is."

Father stretched, reaching his arms high over his head, then twisted his body around on his hips, easing tension from his muscles. He turned his head as far as it would go one way, then the other, twirling it round when he brought it back to face forward. Seemingly more relaxed, he picked me up for another kiss and cuddle.

"Well, you know what I think, Father," said Jake. "That's why I've ended up living like I do. Peace of mind is absolutely priceless, that's what I say. No one can ask any more from you if you follow your soul."

Father's reply trailed off into a near whisper: "You might well be right, Jake, you might well be right..."

"I wish you well, Father, however you decide to take things forward. You'll have my thoughts."

"Thanks, Jake. I'll be alright, don't you worry about me. My, this one is a little cutie, isn't he?"

With one final rub of the ears, Father placed me back down next to Mullet. "Anyway, I'd better go and prepare myself for tomorrow, then get some sleep. You take good care of yourself, Jake. Goodnight."

"Goodnight, Father, God bless."

Father bent down towards me, kissing me softly on the head. I licked his hands in approval before he slipped away through the creaky church door. After he'd gone, I watched the door for a long moment, sensing how the presence of his kindness lingered, then burrowed my way under Jake's overcoat. Someone – Mullet or Jake, I'm not sure which – helped by nudging me into that cosy nest. Snuggled up, enveloped in Jake's earthy smell, lulled by the beating of his heart, muffled from the outside world, I could still distinctly hear Jake speak and, in their repetition, his resonating words became the lullaby that brought peaceful sleep.

"Well, well. Poor Father Cuthbert, eh Mullet? Dear oh dear."

6 FATHER CUTHBERT

Alone in his small, sparse room, Father Cuthbert allowed the silence of St. Peter's night to enfold him. A yucca plant, too big for its pot, wedged by the only chair to prevent it from toppling, dominated the tiny area not occupied by the single bed and basic accoutrements. Christ struggled to peer through the dense foliage from his wall-mounted crucifix. Father Cuthbert did not mind that the Lord was hidden behind the greenery: the plant helped to relax him, transporting his mind back to peaceful days on retreat in the mountains, away from the bustle of the parish, rooting him in nature.

Wearing a simple tunic robe, he settled down into his favoured praying posture. Kneeling, sat back on his heels, back erect, eyes closed, he flexed his head and shoulders this way and that, easing the tension in his tired muscles, then took a deep breath, held it, exhaled slowly. Hands on his lap, thumb tips touching lightly, he felt a bolt of energy course through his arms, into his body, and willed it down to his toes, from where it reflected back up, warming his body. He cleared his mind of the day's fluff and started to pray, not with the Our Father or Hail Mary, nor with rosary beads or mantras, but by allowing the focus on his breath to guide him.

Tonight, however, fatigue overwhelmed him and he struggled to focus on his prayer. Random thoughts coursed into his mind like uninvited boors trespassing a sedate party. He fought off the well-meaning ladies of the parish and dismissed the intrusion of the Church

Bells Restoration Committee Chairman, but the Bishop's presence was more severe. Out of control, his mind ambushed him and he fell into a fitful, restless sleep, so that when he awoke abruptly with the chiming of the alarm clock, still in his kneeling posture, he ached all over.

Outside, it was still dark, but he had to prepare for the 6 o'clock mass. Reluctantly, he levered his body upright and forced himself, stumbling, into the closet bathroom. He swallowed two painkillers. Finally, the new day slapped him with a cold shower.

PART 2
THE YEARS PASS

7 THE CITY

Ah!

You're back again. It's good to see you looking so fit and healthy.

Well, what do you think? Has the city changed at all these last five years?

What?

You can see some new roads on the outskirts.

Come higher with me, then. That's better. What do you think now? How does it compare?

I thought so: it looks identical, doesn't it?

What you need, my friend, is to develop some perspective.

8 THE STREET

Constant vigilance was a burden for an old man of God. The weight of the years had ambushed St. Peter and he had fallen into a years-deep slumber. Not such a long time in the context of the two millennia of his watch but, perhaps, crucial now that the pace of life was accelerating.

Waking up, St. Peter slowly surveyed the street anew.

You can't beat the old adages.

Nothing ever changes, yet nothing's ever quite the same.

Viewed from his lofty steeple, the city looked the same as five years ago. The same bustle, the same noise, the same traffic, ceaselessly pounding this way and that – some would say aimlessly - round the city. St. Peter could see it, could hear it, could smell it. The skyscape too, that was the same. Clearly, there wasn't either the business or the public motivation to build new showpiece buildings in this time of financial stagnation and risk aversion. In the far distance towards the centre, he could still see the castle towers and the tall trees of its park, still see the ugly, functional financial skyscrapers and the stanchions of the stadium, built with the forlorn optimism that heralded the millennium.

And yet…

If St. Peter focused, if he looked attentively at the street, then he could see that the changes were indeed significant, if not fundamental. Disturbed by conversations overheard in his transept, St. Peter had undertaken a more scrupulous surveillance of movement in the street. And now he was certain. There were many more eksterlanders living there - coming and going, children in tow - than previously. What had predominantly been an area populated by citizens was now sullied by these people of uncertain origin.

Cogitating slowly – it was the most that he could muster - St. Peter began to make sense of the disparate pieces of information that he had managed to gleam from his spying. It was like trying to piece together a complex jigsaw puzzle, only further complicated by the fact that some of the pieces were missing.

Yes, I can see it now.

The city was being covertly invaded by eksterlanders. He had heard Father Cuthbert and the Bishop mutter something about a war in the south. Were the people who had arrived in the street refugees from there? Or were they simply economic migrants?

It didn't really matter because they must all be Tembusi. The difficulty of finding places of worship meant that holy churches were being desecrated.

Yes, desecrated!

St. Brigit's, barely a couple of miles away on the wind, had been struggling to keep up its attendance, even on Sundays. Weakened, she had fallen prey to the Tembusi and was now a kroda.

The thought of this terrible heresy caused St. Peter to shiver to his stones, shaking his foundations and causing the bells in his steeple to shimmer in sympathy.

All down the street, people lying awake in their beds were startled by the unearthly, spooky whistle blowing in the night air.

And what, St. Peter pondered, did that mean for Christ? Had St. Brigit's been ransacked? If Christ had been present in the Eucharist in

St. Brigit's tabernacle, as indeed St. Peter believed He was present in his own, then what had happened to Christ when the church had been overrun by the Tembusi and the tabernacle destroyed?

Such profanity.

Had Christ - or a part of Him - been killed? Surely not. Had He run away? Perhaps He had escaped just before the final blow had been dealt and attached Himself to another constituent part in another Eucharist, or elsewhere. St. Peter was confused, his steeple amuddle. His thoughts alarmed him and he shivered again.

His bells quivered, sending another shudder through the sleepless population of the street.

Come on, where's my faith? Gotta have faith. But it's been so long. I am tired and dusty. I thought You were coming back again soon. You promised!

What was clear was that the Tembusi had encroached on the street. Its demographic had changed, bringing the infidel to within a footfall of St. Peter's own steps. And yet there had been no violence that he had seen, no commotion, nothing to unduly alarm him. The street was usually peaceful and quiet, which probably explains why he had not initially noticed the fundamental changes. It was true that attendances for mass at St. Peter's had dwindled, but he had attributed that to the passing of Father Cuthbert's honeymoon period. Now he realised that the incursion of these Tembusi was also a factor. The Catholics had fled.

St. Peter's fury grew at the realisation of what was truly happening.

Outrageous! Why, in that case, have I heard Father Cuthbert preach reconciliation and friendship with the Tembus community? Preposterous! Appeasing coward.

His bells rumbled with anger.

Whoever thought that church bells could emit such a body trembling bass? Not the sleepless residents of the street, who quaked with fear and pulled their duvets over their heads.

How can we hold back the advance of the enemy if we are welcoming them with open arms and preaching friendship? Steadfastness, tradition, observance of ritual. Faith. These are the values that will defeat the enemies of Christ, not woolly-thinking compassion.

St. Peter was in despair. Father Cuthbert had always been a soft touch, always been too keen to do good. There was that smelly tramp, for instance, the one with the mangy dogs that he kept letting into the church at night, despite the protestations of many parishioners, when he thought that no-one was looking.

And, other than St. Peter, no-one was.

Desolate, St. Peter felt chilled to his stones. Hoar frost formed on his capitals, astonishing Jake, who had awoken with the intense cold, not only because of its crystalline beauty, but on account of its miraculous appearance inside the church.

Abandoned!

St. Peter felt that he had been abandoned. In these depraved modern times the Government, obsessed with influencing the millions that the Church could no longer hope to reach, was more interested in manipulating the media. Never mind the Government: he could not even rely on his own parish priest. He felt lost, lonely and abandoned, surrounded by a jumble of tortuous mental noise. Marooned, just like the street.

I believe in You, Christ. Do You still believe in me? Have I been abandoned here? I feel so alone.

Feeling totally devastated, St. Peter trembled mightily to the depth of his foundations.

And, in the street, the suffering sleepless sat upright in their beds, their minds and innards in turmoil at the tumult of bells jangling in the night.

9 SURVIVAL

The years I spent with Mullet and Jake were idyllic. It could be tough to survive without a permanent home, particularly in the winter, but the companionship and love the three of us shared helped to get us through each day.

We did a fair bit of walking, that's for sure, searching out food and shelter, but we also spent long periods of time simply sitting and thinking, or observing the world, pondering its imponderables. We could spend hours simply staring in wonderment and joy at the constantly changing landscape of the sky. People-watching: that too was a favourite pastime, especially enjoyable when we were spending time in the city.

Jake had a special way with other people. Everybody seemed to like him. I don't mean passers-by in the street. If we happened to be sitting in a shop doorway in the early evening, say, they would usually curse, swear or spit. Exceptionally, someone would say a kind word or drop a coin at our feet. Framed by a doorway, Jake would always be treated like a beggar or a tramp. Of course, he was neither of those things. To avoid the aggravation we didn't often rest in those kinds of places, despite the fact that they did provide some shelter and that we often passed them on the 'pizza run'.

The 'pizza run' was one of our favourite ways of getting food when we were in the city. Jake seemed to know every waiter in town. We would wend our way round the backs of the restaurants, loiter in the alleyways where the staff came out for their smoke and he would engage them in conversation. Politics, the war, football, that sort of thing. Mullet and I would put on our 'cute look' and the prize would invariably be leftover pizza or a tub of pasta with sauce.

Not a very healthy diet, I hear you say. Well, I can tell you that keeping up with the latest healthy eating craze was certainly not high on the list of our priorities. When we found ourselves in the city, we ate what we could muster either through Jake's persuasive ways or by rummaging in bins for scraps. Supermarket yards were a good source for those although we were limited as to what we could take because Jake was fussy about what he would or wouldn't eat and only had his primus to cook on. Their large bins would occasionally provide emergency shelter in wet or cold weather. Jake avoided using them though. His small torch was impotent against the impenetrable darkness once the lid was down and that, combined with the stench, was enough to always trigger scary flashbacks of when I was trapped as a pup. I'm sure that Jake could sense my anxiety. He was always very considerate towards Mullet and I.

I've never been sure why but whilst it was clear that Jake had favourite places to rest, it was rare that we slept in the same spot on consecutive nights. Always, always on the move. Why was it that, in the winter, we did not settle in the hospital tunnels for good? The service tunnels were vast – a proper labyrinth – with a myriad rooms for all manner of purposes leading off them. We knew the quieter areas that allowed us peaceful rest fairly well and rarely had to scamper quickly to avoid detection. In freezing weather, heavy rain or snow, the tunnels provided the best shelter. Trouble was, I guess, that there was no food supply down there; perhaps that's why Jake never made it a permanent camp.

In any case, we were all always happier to be outside, able to see the sky and so, out of preference, we would inevitably be drawn to areas where we were closer to nature. Even when we were in the city, we would spend a lot of time in the large park surrounding the castle.

Outside of the city life was different but no easier. Occasionally we would forage. Blackberries, mushrooms, leaves, nuts and more all provided plenty to eat in the right season. The big country park on the outskirts was one of our favourite places in the spring and summer. Not only were there edible mushrooms in the woody areas away from the paths for Jake, but there were always lots of juicy rabbit droppings – such a delicacy - for Mullet and I to feast on. On the week-ends and school holidays, all the picnicking families were dupes for the 'cute look', so we gorged on sandwiches and cake whilst Jake found enough in the waste bins to satisfy him.

We were fortunate when the spring turned sunny and hot. The sun on our backs was the tonic we needed, an infusion of primordial strength. Suddenly, with the soul-piercing, bitter cold banished, night-time ceased to be such a burden, and instead we revelled in the wonder of the sparkling, dew-dazzled world of the sharp early morning light.

Traipsing out into the open from our sleeping quarters, marvelling at our paw prints on the wet grass, we took delight in the magical misty landscape of dawn. Out where the wood gave way to grassy fields the daisies still lay asleep, their petals clenched tight around their eyes, shielding out the sunrise, waiting for warmth. Glistening with the rising sun they played a sky of sparkling stars to the planets of buttercups and dandelions. The dawn chorus over, even sound was subdued, as if respectful of its beauty. At this time of day the distant rumble of traffic was more easily assuaged by the stream. For a brief moment, a peace like no other. We would tread slowly, softly, in awe at the majesty of this inverted universe, afraid to break the wondrous spell of dawn. Further ahead, tufts of rabbit fur, leftovers from the previous evening's buzzard strike or the night's fox kill, were now encased in tiny droplets of water and, caught in radiance, were transformed into scintillating galaxies, surrounded by the twinkling daisy bead-stars atop the grass. The cobwebs, too, were a marvel. Up high they shone like beacons, punctuating the scene with iridescence; on the ground they were transformed into fluffy balls of candy floss.

As the sun continued to climb, so would the hunger in our bellies. Jake would soon be wanting to prepare breakfast. Mullet and I were well practised in what we had to do at this hour to avoid a skimpy meal of stale leftovers and virtually inedible scraps: rabbits! Mullet was an expert rabbit catcher. As soon as I had matured from puppyhood she had enlisted me to assist in the early morning hunt. She'd lie in wait near the entrance to the burrows while I circled far around them. When she was ready - and the funny thing, thinking about it now, is that I always knew when she was ready - I would storm the rabbits, who would be enjoying what they thought was an idyllic, peaceful breakfast. Then, sensing, feeling, hearing – whatever – onrushing danger they would bolt for home. Wrong! Mullet would pick out one, leap out, sprint, bat it with her paw, stunning it, then pounce and break its neck. Absolutely terrifying, the blurry finality of it, the terrible transition from relaxed grazing to cold and calculated demise.

Death.

No more.

No more soft, sweet grass, no more warmth from family.

No more.

After the kill, I would always be very subdued, sitting very still and looking on at Mullet from a distance. She would sniff the rabbit, give it a lick, then gently pick it up in her jowl and carry it back towards me.

The very first time she did it, I wasn't sure what to do, but she showed me by repeating the gesture. I too had to sniff and lick the rabbit. It was clearly a ritual, born out of respect. It was fully a couple of years before I realised that it was a determined attempt to commune and commiserate with the rabbit's departing spirit.

Eventually, Mullet would pick the rabbit up again and walk funereally back to Jake, ears and tail drooped. She would carefully place the rabbit next to him, he would cradle her face, kiss her on the top of the head and whisper: "Good girl, Mullet." Then, not forgetting me, he would ruffle my fur kindly and I would be rewarded with a 'there's a good little fella'.

Jake would prepare and cook the rabbit for breakfast. Anything we didn't eat would soon be recycled by other creatures in the woods. We would often have mushrooms and various leaves cooked in the fry-up: breakfast could be a real treat.

Mullet and I loved our mushroom picking excursions. There was a truly magical place just up where the woodsman's vehicles had long ago forged a path of sorts through the Christmas tree plantation. The abandoned trees grew tall and dense, allowing little sunlight to filter through: this was a damp, cool world even on the hottest days. Mushrooms abounded amidst the luxuriant mossy woodland carpet. Jake seemed to know exactly what he wanted from the myriad shapes, colours and sizes available, homing in on specific types even when they were barely visible amongst a huge clump. He'd be there ages, looking, cutting, bagging. We'd leave him to it and go off into the mass of trees, into the dense undergrowth, hoping to put up a bird, a rabbit or - if our luck was in - a deer. Then we'd be off, chasing excitedly, yipping on our way, mindful not to take too long or Jake would holler himself hoarse when his work was done. Sometimes he could be a tad impatient: surely he realised we were only having some fun and would soon be back.

We weren't always lucky enough to have rabbit for breakfast: there were days when Mullet failed to catch a flighty animal. There were no guarantees in this life of ours. The success of each day depended on our wits and a large slice of luck. It was the same for the rabbits and other beings. Seeing their continuous struggle for food and shelter made us all the more aware of our own good fortune when we had it.

The country park was good for shelter too. The bandstand on the grassy plain was built atop a big storage area where deckchairs and the like were kept. Jake knew how to pick locks and, as a result, we often slept in there at night during the warmer seasons to avoid the long walk back into the city. Another good place for sheltering - a bit airier than the bandstand but a good alternative whenever someone had beaten us to that resting spot – was the folly that stood over the crest of the summit. The hill dropped away steeply from there, offering a fabulous view of the city beneath.

This was a favourite spot for us to sit and observe the world after the weekenders and lovers had decamped elsewhere. From this vantage point the cityscape fascinated me. Juxtaposed with the hill, the woods and the rolling sky ahead, it just seemed so insignificant. All these roads, plus the motorway skirting it to the north, always busy with cars, some going this way and others that. Where were they all going? Would it not save energy if those going north, say, just stayed put, and found a way of contacting those already there to do for them the things that they were making the journey for? In return, they would reciprocate the favour for those of the north – who clearly badly wanted to go south for something or other - so that everyone actually stayed where they were and everything got done. What a load of time and energy they would save. They could then sit and observe the world like the three of us did. I'm sure they would all be as fascinated as we were by all of its wonders. I concede that we ourselves did move about a little bit, as a necessity to find food and shelter, but this ceaseless shifting of to-and-fro traffic seemed a bit ridiculous.

And the traffic was noisy too. Even from that distance, it made a sound, a whispering susurrance like the gabbling of the brook in the woods. At a certain point on one of our routine walks - I always felt that it was almost a surreal spot - the sound of the brook and of the traffic matched each other, merged into one. Mullet and I always insisted on sitting at this enchanted spot, bodies close together so as to get the best effect. Move your head slightly one way, listen intently, and you would pick up the brook, its sweetness dominating the soundscape. Tilt ever so gently the other way and the rushing sound was that of flow of cars and lorries, not water, scurrying past.

Flow of water, flow of traffic, flow of energy: each on its own perpetual cycle. The water would return as rain and then come cascading down again. Were they the same molecules rushing past that spot of the brook as five years ago? It was water, and water is water, isn't it? But the molecules were probably not the same ones. So was the brook the same or was it always different? Similarly the people would return on their ceaseless commute, again and again. But were they the same? Had they not shed some skin, some hair, and had there not been new growth? New cells, new molecules, new parasites, different energy. Their minds would have experienced many different events, many different sensations. So: were they the same people? Or not?

Eventually, Jake would become fed up of waiting for us and, with a loud, peremptory call, jolt us from our reverie.

Seen from the folly, the frenetic city activity reminded me of the ant's nest I'd seen in the woods. Mullet and I had come across it quite by chance. We had been nibbling rabbit poop and sniffing for badger and deer when I nearly bumped into it, nose to the ground, following a trail. The nest mound was enormous, standing at least twice as high as me, taller than Mullet even. Its surface was alive with ants. I scratched at it a little with my paw and it caused a tremendous kafuffle of activity, with ant citizens rushing frantically to repair the damage I'd done. There weren't that many ants close to the nest where I stood; instead, the ants kept to strictly demarcated lines of traffic – ant motorways – and huge numbers were travelling away from and towards the nest. The similarity to the city was striking. It occurred to me that either there really was some method to humans' baffling ways or they were little better than ants. I couldn't make up my mind which was right though.

I distinctly remember – it's one of my clearest and most frequently recalled memories, and I shudder every time that it springs to mind – the feeling of power that I experienced looking at the ant's nest. Smaller I might be, but I imagined vividly that I only had to jump on it, start scratching and scrabbling furiously like I knew I could, and I could send the little blighters hurtling through the air, shrieking ant-screams in their death throes as they were scattered by my manic digging, landing in panic adrift of their scent-roads, lost amongst the undergrowth, far from their companions and home, abandoned to the whims of chance.

Jump. Bite. Stamp!

I could have decimated the nest if I had wanted to. I had the capability. And yet…

And yet…

The thought of such wanton devastation rendered me motionless, as if I had been ossified. Why hurt, maim, kill, sever relationships? Why disrupt these industrious creatures, working so hard to survive the rigours of the world in a not dissimilar way to Jake, Mullet and I?

Just then – it's hard to describe the feeling exactly – a surge of empathy swept through me, resonating within my body, bouncing repeatedly from my tail to my muzzle, swirling through my legs, sparking down my spine, altering my state of mind. My hair stood on end and I felt buoyed up, as if floating, yet the ant's nest remained static relative to me, so I reasoned that I must have still been stood on the ground. Held rigid in awe at this surge of sensation, my awareness of the ants was enhanced. It felt as if I could detect each and every one on the nest, on their motorways all around, within the nest even. I could feel their rhythm, their energy. In some mysterious way, I had somehow been assimilated into their realm.

The reverberation faded and my perception gradually returned to normal. Mullet was sat very still a few yards away, observing me intently without intervening. As I came out of torpor she came up close and licked my nose in friendly greeting. At that moment I knew that she had experienced something very similar, if not identical, in her own past.

How? How did I know that with such certainty? But I did know.

From that day on I always took the greatest of care when in the woods – and elsewhere - to avoid as much as possible trampling on other living creatures.

Ha! I know what you're thinking. 'Hypocrite. How does that measure up against you chasing and killing rabbits?'

Good question! It's one that troubled me often as I sat or lay ruminating on the world. And I'll be honest with you: I never did find an answer that completely satisfied me, but we never stopped the killing. Mullet and I rationalised the situation by virtue of the fact that we needed to eat to survive and that the rabbits had a chance to escape. It was never an uneven contest: the rabbits' speed against our wits and guile. A kill was by no means a certainty. As I've already pointed out, some days we would go hungry for breakfast, the rabbits safe in their burrows. And we never took more than we needed.

Chased them for the fun and joy of the game? Sure, but even the rabbits understood the distinction between play and deadly threat. Call it practice, not play: each of us honing our skills for the serious chase of the dawn.

All around us I observed the same pattern: other conscious beings struggling to find food and shelter, continuously battling against adversity, grateful for any good fortune that came their way.

Survival: that really was a hard task – for all of us out there.

10 AN OBSESSION

Mimi was never far from my thoughts through all the remaining years of school. I had become obsessed after the encounter at her house. Fate seemed to propel us together when, just a few weeks after I had gone flying off my roller skates, I did sufficiently well at school to be promoted up to the top academic class: her class.

And now, there she was daily, free to be gawked at by this silent admirer, who was constantly casting fantastical daydreams of everlasting requited love.

I was frightened to approach her directly, fearful of rejection, for I had never made friends easily and felt awkward away from a small group of quiet boys who similarly shunned attention-seeking feats of bravura. So, for a long time I remained a distant observer, simply longing; the feeling projecting a shadow of anxiety across my mind.

You see, I'd discovered by painful experience that being as unassuming and anonymous as possible was the best policy to adopt to survive school in my own particular circumstances. I'd been picked out for attention by the bullies from the earliest days. I felt like a social outcast, blessed with no qualities whatsoever.

I was an easy target: my name was foreign. Miguel Alves. Under playground law, this crime alone was ample justification for verbal and physical intimidation. I'd tried to avoid the hassle by disguising my name as 'Michael' or 'Mike' even prior to my teens. This was successful to a certain degree, able to fool all but the cleverest of bullies, but the stratagem was ultimately doomed to failure. The other big giveaway was the fact that my skin was naturally a light olive colour, definitely darker than the other boys' and, especially so in the winter, an obvious brand of alienness.

"Dago!"

"Wop!"

"Tembus scum!"

"Spotty git!"

"Four eyes!"

As if an olive-skinned Miguel Alves wasn't burden enough, nature had rewarded me with bad skin and poor eyesight, giving the strong, truculent, blonde boys yet another - in their all-knowing eyes - legitimate justification for attack.

They would surround me, towering inches higher, jostling and goading, hoping to provoke me to say or do something that would trigger the unleashing of some violent act. I'd schtum, try to remain silent and calm, whilst they'd shower word-spittle into my face from bellowing too close, jab at my chest or give me a sharp wedgie.

"Come on, Alves, you Tembus cunt. Take your glasses off so I can smash your face against that wall!"

Ever the gentlemen, never hit a person wearing glasses. What gentlemen! The etiquette of the playground. These toughies, the Knights of the Schoolyard.

I wasn't a Tembus, of course. Well, my parents weren't, to be exact. They'd come from a Catholic land and were branded with that tag despite the fact that mum only seldom went to mass and my father never did. He professed himself an agnostic. As he had ultimate control I wasn't forced to go and rarely accompanied mum.

Eventually, tired of not getting a response, the bullies would wander off on their quests, seeking juicier targets, leaving me with a few bruises and the heavy weight of worthlessness.

I should have been grateful - had I been wise enough to realise it at the time - for my parents' foresight in sending me to a Catholic school, where even the bullies had the conscience not to inflict crippling bodily wounds on someone as puny and scrawny as me. Indeed, I now suspect that aspect had been a crucial factor in their decision but I gave them no credit for it at the time. Instead, I blamed them for creating the conditions that led to me being picked out as different. Well, they were responsible, were they not? Did they not send me away every school holiday to spend time in their native land with my uncle's family? Not only did this scupper any attempts to develop meaningful friendships outside of school, but it also continually emphasised my feeling of separation. I wanted to belong here - they sent me there.

My low self-confidence vanished completely when, at the end of my first term in her class, Mimi refused to dance with me at a school ball. Her rejection was as unexpected as it was devastating. We didn't speak very often due to my natural shyness, but I had observed that she was also shy and kept to a small circle of friends. I was sure she didn't have a boyfriend and so I'd expected her to say yes: in my frequent daydreams this had been the start of a happy relationship.

Very carefully, I picked the right moment to sidle away from my own friends without being observed and felt confident as I approached the group of girls she was standing with, chatting and dancing, in one of the corners of the hall.

"Hi, Mimi, would you like to dance with me?"

"No!" she cried out alarmed, sparking the attention of everyone close by. "I don't."

The world folded in, turned inside out. Vision faded as my brain shrivelled with the shock of rejection. I reeled away without any further words, headed in a random direction, trying to quickly distance myself from her vicinity, seeking anonymity in a more distant part of the hall.

Alone in a dark corner, I recomposed myself, struggling to comprehend why I'd been subjected to such total rejection when so many others seemed to be having a good time. After a while I made my way back to my friends, who were clustered in a quiet, unassuming group. They seemed as absurd within these joyful and buoyant surroundings as my offer of a dance had appeared to Mimi.

I was left mentally devastated by the rebuff. In some respects, it was fortuitous that the ball had been held at the end of term. The ensuing enforced time away from home at my uncle's villa meant that I could wallow in my silence, running unanswerable questions and permutations through my mind, festering in my dejection.

Why had Mimi refused to dance with me? Did she hate me? Had I misinterpreted coy, half-given smiles, or surreptitious glances, discovered then quickly curtailed? There had been no sense of animosity before this, no avoidance of personal space in corridors or in class whenever fate - manipulated by me over countless mental calculations - had brought us into proximity. How could this have happened? Was it purely her natural shyness that wouldn't allow her to accept in front of her friends? Would accepting have broken her unwritten clan code? I hadn't seen Mimi or anyone in her group dance with anybody else.

There must be hope there then, surely. It's not as if I have a rival.

Peace of mind returned slowly during the holiday so that, by the time I returned to school for the autumn term, I had regained my previous composure, such as it was. I resumed normal life - as I knew it - sticking close to my circle of friends, attempting to avoid the pitfalls of the bullies, and constantly observing Mimi.

A couple of years passed. My obsession with her remained unabated. Our interactions continued at a random level subtly enhanced by my trickery. The incident at the ball had never been mentioned by either of us but I certainly lacked the confidence to repeat the approach at any other school ball, or to ask her out on a date. I'd walk nonchalantly past her house, pretending I was going somewhere, sneaking a look, hoping to catch a glimpse. These machinations fuelled my daydreams and my hopes although, strangely perhaps, Mimi never became an object for my masturbation. I'd elevated her to a far higher plane than that attained by mere sexual gratification: I was convinced that I was in love.

Pure love.

Eventually, of course, the temptation to approach her again became irresistible. After all, she hadn't been nasty to me during school time, not unlike some of the other girls who taunted me with their sniping remarks and aloof attitude.

My plan, despite being meticulously formulated over a long period, was straightforward. I would stride up to her front door oozing confidence, ask if she'd like to walk around the park with me, beam with delight at her acceptance, and float into heaven.

I knew that it had to be done.

My plan must be carried through!

Every fibre of my body screamed: "Do it! Do it!" Even so, when the time came for action, the very same fibres that, in my secluded nest, had all aligned in unison in favour of action, suddenly buckled, rendering my legs weak and incapable of carrying my weight to her door. My stomach would turn somersaults, so that I felt queasy and constantly needing the bathroom. My mind was in turmoil, thoughts swirling and spinning. I was incapable of coherent thought.

These reactions were debilitating, but the urge to act remained immense.

Does any being know the number of times that I set off, inspired to act by the desire for pure love, only to fail at the last hurdle? Even the universe has lost count. Where was the fatal decision reached? Which footstep failed? Which was the critical juncture at which my body, rebelling against the wishes of my brain, decided to walk hurriedly on past the house as if I was really on my way to a friend's house or on a shopping mission? Why could I not turn into the drive and knock at the door, as I had envisioned countless times in my mind? Why, why, why? Was I not in any way in control of my own actions? Surely I could perform these simple moves that were etched in my brain: turn into drive, knock at door. Mimi would then answer, as ordained by destiny.

Hi Mimi, would you like to walk in the park with me?

Oh, hi, Michael, yes I'd love to.

Clearly, life itself wasn't so simple. It must have been many months before all the aborted run-throughs of the subroutine embedded in my mind managed to stumble upon a synapse combination that swerved my right leg to the left, tilted my body round and pointed at Mimi's front door. A few short steps more and there I stood, on the hallowed step, heart pulsating wildly, my muscles dysfunctional to the point that I could barely draw breath, let alone speak. Nevertheless, the mental programming now took over and I rang the doorbell, then stepped back to wait for the door to open and my love to appear.

A shadow became visible through the glazing of the front door, taller and larger than I had anticipated. The door opened to reveal Mimi's father, Mr. Tennyson. This was not what I had envisaged. I had no program to deal with this situation.

"Oh, hi, Michael. Are you alright my young friend? What can I do for you?"

Stammering was the best I could muster: "Hi, M-Mr. Tennyson. I was wo-wondering if Mimi was in? Could I sp-speak to her please?"

"Ah, sorry Michael, she's not. She's gone down to that Riverside House place, you know. The care home. She's gone with Catherine to take some of the old folk out for a walk."

"Oh, OK. Thanks, Mr. Tennyson."

Abruptly, I turned to go, unsure of what else to say, unable to cope with the chasm between the reality of the situation and my fantasies.

"I'll tell her that you called, Michael."

"Thanks."

This may seem odd to you, but the simple fact that she wasn't at home when I called seemed to me like another rejection of the most bitter kind. Had I not planned this for months? Had I not suffered excruciating anxiety in order to bring my plan to fruition? Was this not the event that would unite us in a life of unsurpassed love and devotion? How could she fail to be at home?

The repercussions were very similar to those following the debacle on the dance floor of a few years before. I retreated to a quiet place - to my room - and immersed myself in music, attempting to abate the swell of uncontrolled, random thoughts that led to despair. I don't know if Mr. Tennyson kept his promise and mentioned my visit to Mimi; there was certainly no indication from her at school that she knew of it, no meaningful looks or reciprocal approach from her to me. It was rejection, plain and simple.

I felt like a fish in a tank, looking out through the glass at the world sweeping by in all its glory. Nothing that I could do seemed to touch it. Nothing that I did seemed to influence it. I certainly did not understand it. There I was, staring at it, mouth open, agog at its beauty; but its beauty shunned me. My plans, desires, my loves thwarted without effort. There, in my tank, I thought my thoughts, trying to wring some sense from the murkiness that enfolded me.

But I was a fighter and I survived.

Life's early setbacks: Mimi's snub, the bullies, the overbearing parents and the feelings of alienation all instilled within me a mental strength like a shiny carapace, able to reflect the world's woes back onto itself. After a short while, the pain of Mimi's second rejection had abated to a dull ache. It did not carry the fearful force of the dancefloor denial: *no!* This is what the world had in store for me. I could take it. I had become fatalistic, accepting of reality. Sure, I still had feelings, still desired Mimi's love, but I developed a sense of mental detachment that allowed me to view that desire as though it belonged to another entity, so that when the disappointment came it could be deflected back there. Pain? Yes, the entity is feeling pain.

In this way, life became like a role playing game. I acted out what was expected of me. Get up, breakfast, go to school, homework, go to bed: just as father dictated. End of lesson, spill out into the playground, kick a ball about, scream and shout: exactly as my friends would do. I had melded into the environment like a chameleon. I had become virtually invisible to the world.

And yet, just as the fish stares out beyond the tank - *and dare you say he wonders not?* - or as the actor on the stage seeks out the expressions of his ardent admirers in the front rows of the stalls, so I too looked out at the world from my carapace and wondered if - *or was it a yearning?* - I could flip out of my protective shell, join in and become a part of it.

Academic success was certainly an element of that reaching out. Whether through nature or nurture I developed an ability to perform well at sciences and mathematics at school. I liked sciences and maths. Here was cold, calculated result, here was method, technique and answer, right or wrong, not the baffling problems posed by life and love. And there was praise from the teachers at school. Compliments were unusual for me, and generated a good, warming feeling. My father seemed to think that this success was all down to him, taking bombastic pride whenever I scored good results and sickeningly spurring me on to greater effort. More positively, my friends – all the quiet ones, remember - also did well academically, reinforcing the bond between us, so I did have some warmth of friendship down adolescent years.

Perhaps, then, there might be a life for me outside the tank after all.

11 A BATTLEGROUND

Maturity and the approach of university brought a girlfriend. No, not Mimi, but some girl from a lower year with a crush who made a pass at me. Can you believe it? Very gratifying it was too. The relationship lasted about a year. The best thing about it from my perspective was that, towards the end, I thought that it might be making Mimi slightly jealous.

Julie and I were walking back to the bus stop after a movie when we bumped into Mimi and some of her girlfriends. It was either one of those bizarre, random occurrences or pure predestination. Whichever, there was no avoiding my embarrassment at being seen with my arm around another girl. I felt as though I had been caught cheating on Mimi, despite the fact that she had rejected me twice and that we'd exchanged little more than pleasant formalities over the years.

"Oh, hi Mimi!" I said, feigning jollity. "You OK? This is Julie."

"Hi, Julie. Lucky girl."

And that was it. She was gone without another word, lost into the night. Julie and I walked on, she beaming happily, me dumbstruck. The encounter took no longer than a second, perhaps two. It was yet another of those implo-explosive life moments that played havoc with my mind. It was Mimi that I wanted on my arm, not Julie. 'Lucky girl.' What was all that about? Those words would haunt me. Had I lacked sufficient resolve, should I have tried yet another direct approach to Mimi? Perhaps, but, despite my mental carapace, the thought of one more rejection had been too difficult to bear and so I had satisfied myself with brief, inconsequential chatter and the occasional flirty glance - *or was I exaggerating in my mental cooking?* - from Mimi.

The fact that Mimi and I ended up going to the same university was purely coincidental, although I often wondered if it was a sign that fate's calligraphy would eventually unite our names together as one.

No, surely too fanciful, the stuff of silly fairy tales.

I have no idea why she chose to stay in the city. For my part, it was mainly pressure from my parents, particularly from my overbearing father. Keeping me close, keeping control. Perhaps not trying harder to move away was a cowardly stance but, as I had already learned many times in my short life, taking the path of least resistance was often also the least painful. I didn't have the courage for the fight nor, in truth, did I have the maturity, because of my relatively closeted adolescence, to survive far away from my cocoon. I did, however, argue for, and succeed in achieving a move away from the parental home.

The digs weren't too far, a couple of miles at most. The house was situated close to the church of St. Peter, in a street where one of my best friends at school had lived before moving to one of the northern universities, so I knew the area well. It was close enough to pop home for mum to help out with washing and the occasional decent meal, but far enough to loosen the oppressive parental bond, and it was within easy reach of the university and the centre.

My first reaction on finding out that Mimi was also staying in the city was delight, but I quickly dampened the new sense of hope, not wanting to foster it and have it broken again. Fine detective work revealed that she had also moved out of home into student accommodation - she would be a couple of miles away from me, across the other side of the centre. But how could we meet? It would have to be by chance, or by manipulated chance, as she was studying an arts course in a different faculty, so our paths were unlikely to cross as regularly as they had in the same class at school. Still, it transpired that she remained without a regular boyfriend - or girlfriend - and I found my thoughts regularly focussing on her.

My new accommodation was basic: a typical student pad. I had my own bedroom; the sitting room and kitchen were shared with two other guys. I never became close to one of them but Seth immediately became a good friend, a confidante even.

Analysing our friendship, I would say that it flourished because we had experienced similar upbringings and difficulties through adolescence. Each of us must have empathised with the other's resilience. Unlike me, Seth was not an eksterlander, but his skin was much darker, revealing ancestors from a continent far away to the east. He was already a second-generation native whereas I had only arrived on these shores as a six-year old: still young enough to think of the city as my home, but always carrying the stigma that my placental blood tainted another land. Seth called himself a Tembus but I never saw him going to the kroda or observing any other Tembus precepts. I had already convinced myself that religion was more to do with clans and cliques than spirituality: Seth cemented that conviction in my mind.

Living in the street was very much as I expected. It was in a poor part of the city, which is what had become of the areas close to the centre. Its residents largely lived in rented accommodation. The majority of households were either students such as ourselves or Tembus families. Some of these were well established but many others were recently arrived refugees from the war to the south. There were a few white - presumably Christian - families too; poorer paid workers that couldn't afford the suburbs.

I knew some of this motley crowd by sight, even if I was not close to them, through the association of my erstwhile school friend. I'd often walked the couple of miles to his house, then go to the local rec for a muddy game of football: the street and its residents had become familiar. I had even been inside St. Peter's a couple of times, on Mimi spying missions, after I had discovered that she would go to mass there sometimes with some of her friends from school who lived locally. For all its diversity, the street had always seemed peaceful and my school friend had seemed happy and well-adjusted, probably more so than myself. I had no hesitation in moving there.

The underlying peace disintegrated in a very crude way one Saturday during the first term, a few weeks after I'd moved in. Seth and I were walking home from a trip into the centre, overloaded with shopping, when, approaching the street, we gradually became aware of a rumbling sound, like that of a helicopter approaching from a great distance. As we neared home the clamour resolved itself into the angry voices and shouts of a large crowd. With all the buildings reflecting the sound, we were still not entirely sure where it was coming from until we'd walked past St. Peter's and turned into the approach to our own street. There, ahead, we could plainly see a mass of people, gathered in the street, flanked by spols, chanting slogans and shaking their fists at the houses.

"OUT! OUT. White homes, our homes. OUT! OUT."

"GO! GO NOW. GO! GO NOW."

"This city. OUR city! This city. OUR city!"

"Eksterlanders OUT! Tembusi OUT!"

Straining to look over the heads of the spols we saw that the crowd was mainly made up of men. It was difficult to tell exactly because the women looked nearly identical. They had all shaved their hair and painted their heads and faces a dark blue. The blueheads' uniform consisted of denim jeans and white T-shirts. Their clothes were torn, seemingly by design, and any bare skin on their legs and arms was covered by tattoos. Blue, of course.

The spols had formed a cordon along the line of parked cars, making the pavement a kind of no-man's land that provided a buffer zone protecting the houses themselves. They were reluctant to allow us to walk on home past the mob. Seth had some ID that proved he lived in the street and they eventually relented, whispering:

"Go on then, hurry and keep low. Get inside, this lot's nasty. We're struggling to get them to move on."

As soon as we'd trotted a few tens of yards, hunched down to avoid being seen, it became obvious that the spols had been right to be concerned. Some of the residents' curiosity had overcome their fear and alarm. Stupidly, they had opened their front doors and were peeping out over the cordon to get a good look at the mob. This just inflamed the blueheads. Even a face at an upstairs window was causing uproar. We caught glimpses of yobbos jumping up and baring their teeth, distorting their features horribly, like a horde of monkeys inciting a rival tribe to a scrap. The noise was frightening, like a physical battering that the spols' barrier could not prevent. Then, the moment we reached what we thought of as the safety of our home, we heard the sound of shattering glass through the hubbub of chants, followed by an intensification in the clamour as the blueheads celebrated the minor victory.

We rushed towards the front door, battering into each other and virtually wedging ourselves in the entrance in our hurry to be inside, then slammed the door shut behind us. The house, this untidy student house, became a haven, dulling the screams of the mob, muffling the concussion of breaking glass, allaying our terror. We flopped down in the sitting room, sheltering behind the sofa, not daring to look up, hoping that our home would not be the target of an attack and that the spols' line would hold.

The demonstration continued. Time stretched. Sound was our only source of information and fuelled our fear. The ferocity of the chanting, the bile of the blueheads. The interval between dull thuds of misaimed rocks hitting walls. The crack of splintered window panes. The celebration of the mob. We cowered under this soundscape of terror like besieged trench soldiers, irrationally too frightened to speak so as not to reveal our position.

The spols prevented the blueheads from breaking through the line. A distant siren brought hope of reinforcements and an end to the impasse. The intervals between percussive, soul-jarring attacks lengthened. The sound of the chanting mob petered out, the terror now either transferred to another street, another neighbourhood or, less likely, the bile of the marchers spent.

After regaining some composure we peeped up over the top of the sofa to try to get an impression of the demonstration, initially too scared to look brazenly out of the window. All we could see was the cordon of spols, still standing firm. As silence re-established its mantle over the street we became bolder, abandoning our barricade and crawling to the window for a better view. The spols had left. The empty street was littered with debris: rocks, discarded placards and other rubbish blowing in the wind.

Desolate, desolate. A deserted, sad wasteland.

We sat there, Seth and I, stunned, the silence between us like a grim funeral. An image that I'd barely seen during our frenzied, crouched run along the pavement now burned itself into my mind: a child's bulging, terrified eyes as her face popped up at a window. The image was haunting and refused to fade, as if seared into my subconscious.

"Fuck," said Seth, as if reading my thoughts.

"Bastards," I said.

12 PERSPECTIVES

The woods were full of places of wonder and intrigue that would always exert their awesome primeval dominance over us, no matter how often we'd experience them.

One such place that always rendered Mullet and I motionless was the Big Tree. Jake had regular routes that he would take day to day, mixing them up but rarely deviating to try anything new. One such route took us on a wide track cut out for the logging vehicles. At one point, about half a mile from the main road, this track wound its bendy way up a steep hill. We'd bow our heads low, struggling against the incline and then, as the gradient eased, look up to get our bearings, only to be confronted by the sight of this massive tree about thirty yards ahead.

Reflecting on that time, I now find it peculiar that, regardless of how often we made our way up that hill, knowing what was to come, the impact was always as strong.

The Big Tree had the widest trunk of all the trees in the woods. Peculiarly, as we continued to trudge on slowly up the rest of the slope, its girth widened with every step. I was transfixed by this expanding giant and would come to a halt, sit, and just stare. Mullet's reaction was identical. Indeed, it seemed to me that from the time that the Big Tree came into view our thoughts and actions seemed to meld into one. Our movement too – even our breathing – was synchronised and we would think for each other. It was as if we became one conscience, one being. As we sat and watched intently, the tree would stop expanding but even so we'd stay there, spellbound, rooted to the spot like the tree itself. Jake would always have to break the trance, hollering out:

"Oi! Come on you two. Get on with it. Come on!"

Reluctantly we'd move forwards once more, slowly, as Jake's frustration reached us on the wind:

"Every time. It's not that steep. I don't see what it is with you two and that spot."

But the really curious part was yet to come. As we followed the rest of the path on up the hill, the Big Tree grew wider and wider and then - as if its structure could no longer cope with its inflated size, or as if it had been suddenly torn asunder by a ray of light - it split audaciously into two straight down the middle, even as we were watching. The Big Tree had somehow miraculously given birth to another!

Urged on by Jake's impatient hollering, we would resist the temptation to stop and stare again, trudging on, eyes never deviating from the two large trees. Mercifully, as the path twisted, they would be hidden from sight. The enchantment was broken. Our minds free once more, we'd accelerate and catch up with Jake just before the brow.

"Ah, there you are. About time."

As we reached the top the vista opened up to a wide expanse of grassland. Muscle and mental tension eased, Mullet and I would break into play whilst Jake, still puffed out, sat and watched from a fallen trunk at the edge of the track.

Mullet might have been an ace at catching rabbits, but was slower than me at play. Either that or she pretended to be; I never could figure it out. I'd have to goad her to get started, leaping and twisting in the air in front of her, then darting in, biting her scruff, quickly sprinting off again. If she didn't follow, I'd go in again, maybe nip her ankles for variety. She'd respond and we'd be off, her chasing me. If she lagged behind then I'd flip into hopping, allowing her to catch up, then twist, dart in for a quick nip and sprint off again. Occasionally she'd manage to trip me up and I'd go rolling through the grass. It was great fun! Eventually, no amount of goading from me would persuade her to respond and we'd trudge back to Jake, panting heavily.

"Alright, kids? That was a fun game you had. Better have a drink now, then we'll be off."

There were yet more mysterious places in the woods. The cloaking foliage played host to a myriad micro-worlds, each with its own physical laws, like the path running east of Eight Acre. That eerie place was where we met the dog wearing sunglasses. I'll tell you about that meeting in a moment, but first things first.

When I was a pup, Eight Acre was just a fenced-in grassy field in the middle of the woods. Saplings had been planted but were struggling against the onslaught of rabbits because some naughty dogs – *not me you understand!* - had seen fit to play 'aeroplanes' with the plastic bark protectors. Nobody looked after the place and it was slowly being recolonised into natural order, wildness creeping ever closer each season. Mullet and I fitted easily through the sheep-wire mesh and loved running through the tall grass, leaping up to see our way. Jake continued on the path around the perimeter of the field and, having had our fun, we would rejoin him.

The section of path running north along the eastern border of Eight Acre was clearly delineated by the erosion of regular use but was only wide enough for one human. About half way along it headed directly towards a tree. This was a fairly plain tree, you understand, nothing to compare with Big Tree the girth-buster. The path did not, as you'd expect, veer slightly to one side or the other to avoid the tree. No – even from a few yards away it aimed straight towards it. Then, just as you were about to clatter yourself on the trunk if you'd stayed on the same course, the path split in two. One part passed to the left of the tree, the other to the right.

'Trivial detail,' I hear you think. 'Why is he even bothering to mention it?'

Well, one day – not a day that had woken up feeling special: no, it felt very much the same as many others – when we were on the path headed for the tree, the realisation struck me hard like a smack on the muzzle that we always – *always!* – passed the tree on the path to its right. Never to the left.

Why?

What was wrong with the path to the left? Why was there not only the one path, so that the choice – and the many questions – would never arise? Why was there a need for two paths? Why did we always go to the right? What would happen if, one day, we passed the tree to the left?

Shivers!

Shivers of dread and fear! Even now my mind quakes with the memory of it.

If we inadvertently slipped to the left, perhaps we would open up a new dimension or a portal to another time, another universe. Be sucked screaming down the plughole of the world. Be flushed through space-time tunnels to rot in a black hole hell. Or perhaps we would break the supernatural spell that was keeping the trees rooted to the ground and unleash giant walking tree-monsters to devastate the city below.

That path to the left was really not innocuous! I sensed that Mullet was feeling the same anxieties as me. Just as with the Big Tree, her body demeanour altered, became cowed even, every time we approached the spot. It became a place of great anxiety whether we were walking in front of or behind Jake. If we were ahead then the moment we were safely past the tree we'd turn and watch his progress.

"Keep right. Keep right!" we'd shout fervently.

"Stop yipping," he'd always reply. It was part of the ritual. "What is the matter with you two? Be quiet."

On the other hand, if Jake was ahead, we would freeze as he approached, tension rising, particularly if he stubbed his toe, wobbled and looked as if he might stray to the left. But no. Thankfully, even if off balance, he would always twist and pass the tree to the right.

Phew… panic over.

Does Jake also worry about taking the left-hand path?

Another very odd facet of the left-right side of the tree conundrum was that if we were walking that path in the opposite direction, as we occasionally did, then the anxiety never manifested itself. I can't even remember ever noticing the same tree, nor could I tell you which side of it we passed.

Strange.

It was along that path – one day when we were walking in the 'safe' direction – that we first met the dog wearing sunglasses. Mullet sensed him first, before he was in sight, and stopped in the middle of the path, blocking the way. I let my senses meld with Mullet's, focussing on her point of interest and scented the dog maybe a hundred yards or so away. He was an old lab cross, quite scrawny looking, and from afar it looked as if he had two huge black eyes. He was trailed by his human, a gaunt woman so thin that you could virtually see through her. She wore a polka dot red scarf covering her hair – *did she have any?* – and she walked with all the care of God the Protector, as if trying to avoid stepping on any creatures that might be hurt. She was so wispy that I doubt if she would have left any imprints on fresh fallen snow.

There was no animosity emanating from the dog so I ran on ahead, tail and ears displaying a friendly greeting. The mongrel returned the welcome, jumping up playfully on the spot. Mullet joined us and we were soon sniffing each other thoroughly, each of us unabashedly allowing access to all the more interesting and intimate areas.

“Anna! How wonderful to see you. It’s been too long,” Jake called out to the woman as they converged on us dogs.

“Jake. My man! Fantastic!”

They hugged and kissed, methinks a little too enthusiastically, and allowed the embrace to linger longer than decorum decreed, so that we felt compelled to turn our backs and pretend to eat rabbit poo, of which there was none.

“You’re looking well,” said Jake when he eventually emerged from the clinch. “A bit thin, perhaps, but otherwise ravishingly radiant!”

“You old flatterer, Jake. Open your eyes. We struggle on, you know, best we can.”

Jake had been right. Her smile was as bright as a warm sunrise, brimming with joy.

Anna continued: “You been avoiding me? Took me ages to track you down. Food for the soul finding you here. How’s you?”

“Yeah, all good. Great to bump into an old friend. And how’s Luke coping? He seems well enough.”

"Oh, he's good. His eyes will never recover, of course, not after what those bastards did to him in there, but he's got used to his glasses. Other than that he's like any other normal dog. Slowing up a bit with old age but aren't we all?"

Jake chuckled. He and Anna had clearly stopped to chat. Us dogs milled about, not going too far out of respect for Luke, who seemed less athletic than Mullet and I.

"Too true, too true."

"You've gained another friend since we last met."

"The little fella? Mullet brought him in as a pup and he's always stayed. Been abandoned I think. Super dog."

"He seems very sensitive. Perceptive even. Look how he is with Luke."

"Yeah, he's clever like that. Fancy a bite to eat? I've some mushrooms."

"Ooh, yum. Please."

They sat on a stump, side by side, bodies touching, the chat easy as warm slippers, whilst Jake unpacked the primus and prepared a snack. As the cooking aroma intensified the three of us approached and sat facing them from the other side of the stove, not exactly begging but certainly raising the pressure with the severity of our stares. Jake and Anna knew they were besieged.

Jake's counter attack was pitifully pathetic: "There's not enough mushrooms for you chaps. We haven't yet done the foraging today. This is just a snack."

"Aw, Jake, you can't. Look at them."

"Oh, alright. Emergency rations it is then."

He stood and delved deep into his rucksack, arms disappearing down the sides. He firkled for a while, grunting continuously, then eventually resurfaced holding a small packet wrapped in tissue.

"This is it, guys. Your emergency rations. Remind me to replenish them soon, OK?"

He unwrapped the packet and placed it carefully by their feet. We shuffled anxiously on our vents. Then, as they ate, Jake and Anna took turns to lob pieces of dried food at us. Surprisingly, Luke was as adept at catching them mid-air as we were: impressive for a dog wearing such dark shades. The three of us never dropped even one.

"Do you ever see any of the others?" Anna asked as they ate slowly, trying to prolong the small meal, savouring every bite.

"Rarely. Best not to mingle too much. Safety in isolation. I think we all think that. You?"

"Same. Occasionally. But we never linger and make sure to change our routine for a while afterwards. I've seen Adam a few times: he's often at the travelling fair in the central park."

"I've seen him there too. He likes his risks. Particularly doing what he does."

"Yeah, but he's also pretty good at cultivating the art of invisibility, when he's not actually there. I mean, where does he go? Have you seen him anywhere else? He doesn't have a dog, so I suppose that makes it easier."

Jake chuckled. It should have been a warm sound but it carried sadness on its fringes, and was followed by prolonged silence, no response forthcoming from his lips. The meal was over. But not only that - the air rippled with the tension that had suddenly arisen between Jake and Anna. Neither wanted; no, to be more accurate, both were too frightened to flow forward with the seconds, realising, perhaps unconsciously, that another pivotal life moment was arriving.

Jake began cleaning and tidying up, the nervousness making him tremble visibly. This typhoon of complex anxiety battered into us dogs, blowing us away. We scuttled off, again busying ourselves with the seemingly obsessive sniffing of damp earth. Jake read our nervousness and knew that there was no holding back the surge of time. He had to break the silence:

"Yeah," but then paused alarmingly. Time slowed, allowing him the chance to catch up and recompose himself before continuing normally. "More lonely though. I've never seen him anywhere other than the park, that's for sure. And the facility? Heard anything?"

"Only that it's still being repaired, even after all this time. Very slow. Arguments about funding, plus there's someone in the senate arguing on our side, that it shouldn't be reopened. On an ethical basis."

"Hmm… progress."

"Of sorts. But the feeling is that it probably won't be enough. Not this time."

"Well, it'll have to be someone else takes action next time. We're all out of it."

"Yep."

The impromptu picnic items were now all back in the rucksack. Anna and Jake stood facing each other. She took his hands in hers and cupped them, caressed them, squeezed them lightly, allowing her warmth to suffuse through and envelop him. Again we three scurried to find fascinating scents, noses to the earth, but the scene was too tempting and I kept sneaking a look.

Anna was forlorn now. "Will we ever dare to rejoin the race, Jake, return to some kind of normality?"

"Can't see it. This is our normality now. They know who we are. Where'd we go? No, I think that life's lost for us."

"But what about us, Jake? Us! We could stick together, us two, just for a while, couldn't we?"

"Makes it more difficult to stay inconspicuous though, Anna. And to survive." They'd been holding hands all the while and then Jake kissed her softly on the tip of the nose before continuing. "We'll see. In the summer perhaps. After the fair. It's possible. 'twould be nice. But not now."

"Jake?" Her voice crackled, uncertain. She was broken. A sparkling crystal shattered into a myriad shards. "How long have we got, Jake? Living this life? It's tough."

"Anna…" Gently, pleadingly said. "We have to wait. You know that. They know who we are."

Her frustration was evident. "On the run, on the run, always on the run. Is there no end to it?"

"You've got to try to make more of it than that, Anna. Take joy from life, from Luke."

"Yeah." Her vocal chords vibrated. The tongue and mouth shaped the word but her spirit was silent. The absence of essence chilled me, the sound of her voice as cold as the space between the stars.

Their mood had deflated me: my ears were drooping and my tail was tucked up tight to my belly. I sat straight and watched intently, not caring now if they saw me staring. They embraced again, holding each other close, eventually parting without more words, stepping back from each other. Each stood perfectly still, seemingly bereft of life, as if about to draw their last breath before plunging off the plank into the fathomless deep.

Luke was the first to react, trotting off without even a lick goodbye. Anna followed him, walking steadily, steadfastly resisting the urge to look back. Jake continued standing where he'd been embracing Anna, transfixed as if the soles of his feet had taken inspiration from the trees and sprouted roots, tethering him forever to that spot. Mullet and I also remained immobile, paralysed by dejection.

Eventually Jake shook himself, shifted his body and donned the rucksack, setting off in the opposite direction to Anna. We soon followed. There was no fooling me: I could see, and sense strongly, his dejected mood. The aftereffect of the encounter with Anna was much more burdensome than the weight of the rucksack. Deep despair coursed through Jake like a rampant plague, leaving him stooped and unable to do more than drag his feet along the ground, scratching a groove on the surface of the earth that would tell the sad truth of their painful parting for months to come.

13 DREAMS

I'm frightened of going to bed, anxious of falling asleep. The aftermath of the demonstration in the street - has it really been six months? - still burns fervently deep in the recesses of my mottled brain.

When light-triggered mental activity slows,
when dusk settles like dust,
when eyelids droop and slam shut from fatigue:
then!
There!

Vivid technicolor 3-D holographic virtual reality quadrophonic sensurround sound.

In the murk of my room and out of the unsuspecting unconsciousness of sleep they come, exploding with the ferocity of the Big Bang reborn.

The dreams!

Is there anything real in the world outside of my brain? Am I going crazy?

I try. Believe me, I try hard to stay awake. It's a battle of wills. Me against my subconscious. I know who will win but still I make the effort because I've already experienced the consequences of defeat too many times. Not good.

I've already been into the kitchen, done that, messed around, talked to Seth till one, clattered around, got told off by the other house-mate for making a noise.

I sit and listen to music but the jangling of my neurons drowns even the bass and drums.

What is life without pleasure in music?

Can't concentrate on anything. Much too tired. Study some more. Bored. Logon, surf some porn, can't get hard, play a game, feel myself nodding off.

Woa! No!

Return to the kitchen. Make cocoa. It makes me feel bloated and slightly nauseous. I stumble back to my room, sit on my bed and stare.

Stare.

Stare? At what?

No images from the room register in my brain, as if the jumble of thoughts pinballing haphazardly inside my skull finds a way to exit through my eye sockets and tramples over any light rays that are hesitatingly trying to enter. Whoever said that light travels in straight lines? The light in my room turns and runs, fleeing from the onrush of tangled thoughts.

So, I continue to stare. Blankly.

I feel exhausted, like a limp lettuce. Imperceptibly, my eyelids close and I lack the strength or the will to force them open. I succumb. Shattered, I undress and crawl into bed, still daring to hope that tonight will be different. It can't go on like this forever.

Can it?

I know it will start with the scared, window-framed girl's face. It always does. She will fade and I will roam, veering off in seemingly random directions, all featuring horrific scenes of depravity being perpetrated by human against fellow human.

Torture and suffering.

Gore and pain.

Weeping and wailing.
I'm very tired...

♦ ♦ ♦

The plane is travelling very low now. We are below the roof level of some of the tallest houses and I can clearly see everything on the surface. We are flying abnormally slowly: it's as if time itself is playing in slow motion. This is all wrong. The plane is going to crash, I know it is. This is where I die. Time is allowing me to savour the precise moment of my death.

I've often dreamt this very scene so I know what is going to happen next. Well, similar scenes to be exact. The details are subtly different but the outcome is always the same. The plane is flying too low and it is nowhere near a runway or safe landing area. There's a fortified wire fence ahead, or a mountain, or a dense forest, or we are ditching into the sea. Panic builds within me as I stare out of the window, desperately willing the plane to rise, to take evasive action. But it never does. In the last fraction of a second before the inevitable impact, I will sit back in my seat and look straight ahead at the back of the chair in front, bracing myself for oblivion.

And then I will wake up, agitated and anxious. The experience is unnerving, even if I've been through the dream before and can half-rationalise that I am safe in my bed just as the end arrives.

Only this time I am certain that it's for real. Everything is very tangible. The dreams have only been a presentiment.

Shit! I am about to die.

Somehow the knowledge of my fate relaxes me. I regain my composure. And so I do what I've always done in the dreams: I stare out of the window at the hyperclear world.

We are flying at an acute angle towards a pot-holed road. Perhaps the pilot is hoping to land there. Some hope: I know how this will end.

I can see children dressed in ragged clothes. There are a half dozen of them, maybe more. They're running along the road ahead of the aeroplane. The movement of their arms and legs suggests they are sprinting as fast as they can. We keep pace with them for a while, not approaching, as if rejoicing in their fear. Yes, fear: I can sense their fear. It is intertwined with my own.

That's it. The children are running away from us. They are terrified of the plane. But how can it be that we are not simply overtaking them? How can we fly so slowly? Yet they're real: I can see them so clearly, even the dust they are kicking up off the road. Then we accelerate, crossing the road directly above them, so low that I see them throwing themselves to the ground, anticipating an impact.

The plane's nose lifts and we rise viciously, then bank steeply back towards the children. My stomach churns with the disorientating acceleration. I grip the back of the seat in front of me and have to yank my face towards the window. I gasp when I see the children again. Their faces are distorted with pain as they stumble forwards, incapable now of running. Soldiers scurry them along.

And there! In their midst, magnified I know not how, is a naked child. I recognise her immediately. She was the girl at the window during the protest in the street. Her skin is streaked with orange. Eyes screaming pain, mouth agape. The personification of total terror.

But how can she be here? I slump back instinctively in shock. My head thumps into the seat rest. As I lean forward to look out again the engine's tone changes up in pitch. I catch a glimpse of trees just ahead. The plane lurches to port, trying to avoid impact. I know it's too late. We're flying too low. The engines scream now but it's no use. The plane bucks and flips downwards like a rollercoaster car.

This is it!

I resign myself to the darkness.

♦ ♦ ♦

I awake suddenly, springing up into a sitting position. I am in my bed, not on the plane. The night is cold but I'm sodden with sweat. My own dampness chills me, making me shiver. I peel away the sheets that cling to my naked body. My unseeing eyes must be wide open in the dark room because I can feel the eyeballs trying to break out from their socket prison. Fumbling for the bedside lamp in my panic, I knock over the glass of water. The clink and splosh sound startles me but then I feel the switch and press it. Dim light hesitatingly imposes itself, pushing back the shadows. Banished, they cower in small cavities, patiently awaiting the chance to reinstate obfuscation and uncertainty. My mind, emboldened by the realisation that this is my room, my space, my nest, begins to establish some order, disentangling the maze of runaway thoughts. I grab my towel, rub myself dry, walk around.

Confidence regained, I open the door fractionally, reach out to flick the light switch and peer out into the hall. Empty, but there's a light from under the kitchen door. One of my house mates is up. I throw on my robe and tiptoe down the hall. It's Seth.

"Hey man, couldn't sleep?"

"Nah: bad dreams. I'll have a cup of tea, wait for daylight, take a snooze then."

"Me too man. I'm way tired though. Everything's so unsettling now. Too much shit going on."

So we sit there drinking tea, not talking but comforted by each other's company, until daylight pulls back night's oppressive blanket. Reassured, we take our cue and, wordlessly, retreat to our pits for a couple of hours' kip.

14 A STORM

The parting from Anna had left Jake emotionally scarred. He seemed totally distraught, devoid of life even, unable to shake off the dejection enveloping him.

We would soon meet Adam, although he wasn't the succour that Jake's soul hankered for after the encounter with Anna. He was, exactly as she had said, at the fair in the vast park which sprawled through the centre of the city, extending from the castle, over the river and all the way to the sports stadium. The park's size and variety of environments made it a popular place for us to frequent when we were in the city. It was to become a pivotal place for me in that life, although I had no inkling of that when we met Adam.

It was a warm and dry spring day. We'd gone to the fair in search of food. Fairs and such like would always provide us with a full belly and were ideal for watching people, a favourite pastime.

On this occasion we were still circulating, not yet gorged, when we came upon a crowd standing in a circle. People were staring intently into the centre of this stage they'd so created. Jake stretched and rose on tiptoe, straining to get a good look over the top. Intrigued, I sneaked between people's legs to see what the fuss was about. There, in the centre of the circle, sat a man with a great bushy white beard, totally still, legs crossed.

At first I didn't understand. What was so special about this man? His beard was just like Jake's: not that interesting.

How stupid! How did I not realise straight away?

He was sat, but on what? He was sat, or appeared to be, on precisely nothing. It was as if he was simply floating there, cross-legged, in mid-air. It couldn't be! A trick, surely. Even I knew that.

A small boy was tempted to challenge his disbelief and ran forward, passing his outstretched arm freely under the man's bottom. Then, as if to prove a point, he lay on the grass and rolled under the floating man. The crowd gasped. The man smiled, a broad toothy grin, and raised his arm, swinging it up and over his head, as if to say: 'Look, no strings.' Not that there was anywhere to suspend him from anyhow.

A soft susurration sifted through the perplexed crowd like a sea swell sweeping its way up pebbles on the beach. People whispered disbelief to their companions. The floating man sensed the changing mood and cunningly brought proceedings to a close. He calmly brushed imaginary crumbs from his thighs, stood up and bowed ostentatiously. The crowd, though unsure, took their cue from this act and applauded, hesitatingly at first but then, finding courage in the sound itself and each others' response, enthusiastically.

"Dad, that man was floating," said the small boy, tugging at his father's trousers.

"Don't be silly, lad. It's just a trick. Good one, though, eh?"

"But dad, there's nothing underneath him."

"It's a trick, son, that's all it is."

When the applause attenuated, the floating man doffed his cap and slowly walked round the unquestioning unbelievers, smiling disarmingly, as though he was the most normal of people. Their alarm assuaged by this return to theatre, most people in the crowd were happy to drop in a coin or two, satisfied after seeing such a clever magic trick.

Jake remained where he was and caught the floating man's eye as the crowd dispersed. He grinned broadly and walked forward in greeting:

"Adam, you old goat! You shouldn't tease people like that. You're meant to be keeping a low profile. You'll get arrested."

"Jake! Fantastic to see you. Ha, ha. It's just a bit of fun. Don't you just love it? There's not one of them prepared to believe what they can so easily see. People are such peculiar things."

"Well, it is unusual, you have to admit. Anyway, how you keeping?"

"Good, good. You? Looking a bit thin there, Jake, you alright?"

"Yeah, sure. All the walking, you know."

Adam began looking through the booty in his cap, smiling broadly all the while.

"Well, generous unbelievers are always better than stingy believers, eh, Jake? This little fella yours? You only had Mullet last time. What say that I treat you all to a sublime banquet of burgers and chips? Veggie ones of course: no meat."

We wagged our tails approvingly at the suggestion.

"Sounds good to me, Adam. If you're feeling rich."

"I'm sure I can get away with another couple of performances later, before moving on and doing my vanishing trick. Let's go feast!"

And so we did. Adam was an affable host. Mullet and I had the luxury of our own portions. We finished well ahead of the men and then lay contentedly nearby whilst they ate and chatted quietly, propped up against some beer barrels.

As dusk approached the two men hugged companionably. I sensed a very deep, if different, connection between them to that which Jake had with Anna. Farewell over, Adam wandered back towards the hubbub of the fair, no doubt to weasel some more coins from baffled crowds, whereas we followed Jake towards the city for our night's rest.

Another very clear memory from that life again stems from one of the times that we visited that same travelling fair.

Jake, Mullet and I had feasted on candy floss and toffee apple. Replete and satisfied, the three of us were sitting on the mound overlooking the fairground and calmly taking in the world.

It had been a sweltering summer's day. As the afternoon faded into early evening large clouds formed on the near horizon, bulbous and tall. They skyscrapered rapidly, menacing heavy rain and were moving towards us at speed with the forcing upper wind. Jake saw and understood the risk. He must have been considering moving us towards shelter but, unusually given the obvious threat, we remained observing the crowds and fair awhile longer.

Many revellers decided to leave early, frightened by the ominous, invading darkness. This great diversity of people passed directly in front of our vantage point in a fascinating procession. Children in prams, children in baby carriers. Haggard old men limping at speed, swinging their gammy legs wildly out in an arc like a scythe. Unwashed youths with wild, untamed hair. Three-generation families, placidly hurrying. The scene was one of general good nature, the mood light. Laughter floated on the wind as the happy fair-folk wound their way back home.

Suddenly something jolted my senses, like a violent electric shock! I jumped up, alarmed. The impression persisted and affected my whole body. The pads on my paws were tingling – vibrating almost – as if the whole earth itself was trembling. My ears shot up, hard and erect. My mane was bristling with the anticipation of something extremely unpleasant. And yet there had been no lightning, nor had the storm arrived over us. Puzzled, I circled and searched for the cause of my trepidation.

There! An extraordinary, vibrant red mist, crackling with static electric discharges.

Ball lightning? Of that size, before the storm even?

When I stared intently at it I realised that it wasn't actually red mist, only the sensation of it, encircling a group of young men hurrying purposefully along. I had to concentrate carefully to make out the youths, such was the shrouding effect of this ethereal mist. It enfolded them as they moved, intrinsically attached to them.

The response to that misty colour resonated within me, as though all of my insides were being twisted violently, forcing me to once again jump up involuntarily on all four paws. I was beginning to feel sick, my tummy churgling irritatingly.

Instinctively, I started to bark furiously at the men but Mullet sensed my anxiety and placed a paw on my back. I quietened and sat back down. Jake shuffled over to put his arm round me, and gently placed his other hand on my chest. I was being cuddled, comforted, but I understood that I was also being restrained.

"Stay, boy, there's a good little fella."

It quickly became clear that the red mist - the men - was beaming towards one of the family groups that was leaving the fair. There were four small children and two adults, who I took to be their parents. The mother's face was covered by a black veil. As the red mist approached the family group, the soundscape of the fair altered dramatically. The warm hum overscored with laughter shifted in pitch as onlookers realised the danger and began to call out warnings. Seeing that the element of surprise was about to be lost, the red mist sprinted towards the group, shouting threateningly and gesticulating, causing children - not just those in the family that was the focus of the charge but others nearby - to start crying and screaming.

Whilst I watched, the misty scene shifted into purple, as if someone had put a colour filter before my eyes. I had to focus intently to be able to see clearly. The shouted obscenities made the youths' vile intent obvious. The father placed himself between his family and the onrushing attackers, arms spread wide, making himself big, protecting his loved ones.

My instinct and intuition was to intervene, to rush forward and act, but I remained rooted to the spot, looking on, struggling wilfully against Jake's firm embrace. It was no use: his restraining pressure was solid. A pitiful squeal was all that resulted from my vain efforts to squirm free.

"Sshhh…"

The youths didn't slow as they neared the man. Two of them simply bundled him over and pinned him to the ground. Another grabbed hold of the woman and locked her arms behind her back. When it became clear what the remaining youth was going to do the intensity of the onlookers' screaming exploded but nothing – *nothing!* - before or since in my lives could have prepared me for the excruciating, piercing yell that erupted from the woman's throat as the lout brandished a blow torch and proceeded to burn away the veil that was covering her face. She squirmed and kicked out frantically but her resistance was futile. The demonic attacker was able to focus the roaring flame, intent on destroying every last vestige of cloth. The smell of barbecued meat suffused the air, making me retch.

The woman's children retaliated, kicking and flailing at the manic youths in a frenzied attack, but they were easily and forcefully pushed off, tumbling to the ground. Eventually, one of the bystanders in the homerushing crowd couldn't tolerate any more and, putting personal safety aside, rushed forward, launching himself like a missile at the flame throwing youth, knocking him to the ground. Emboldened by this display of leadership, others came forward to help. Sensing they would be overcome if they dallied any longer, the two youths holding the father down jumped up, kicked the original bold defender in the head, allowing them all to flee, screaming more insults as they ran.

The woman collapsed to the ground, wailing manically. Fragments of the smouldering veil had become glued to her melted skin. She jabbed at her face, desperately trying to remove the remains of the smouldering garment, frantic to ease the piercing agony. A man rushed forward from the crowd and doused her face with water from a bottle, then helped her husband to prise off the remaining cloth.

The coloured mist had vanished with the youths but it was becoming difficult to see more of what was happening because of the number of people milling around the woman. It was clear that she had been badly disfigured in the attack. The skin had already burst in places, leaving streaks of blood smearing her face. Her children had seen the gross disfigurement and were hysterical. They were running aimlessly round in circles, screaming, and then crumpled together into a heap, sobbing pitifully into the earth.

A first aid team arrived, pushing their way through the gawkers, keen to attend to the woman. At that point, Jake withdrew his arms from around me, scuffled me fondly on the ears and said: “Well, kids, we’ve seen more than enough for today. We need to be going now.”

We obeyed without hesitation, stunned and shocked by what we had just witnessed, slipping away over the back of the mound towards the less populated part of the park, avoiding the crowds, choosing to take the longer road back into town.

My mind felt numb, devoid of thought, unable to shake off horrific images of the blow torch flame and I trotted along dispiritedly behind Jake and Mullet.

The attack itself and its aftermath couldn’t have lasted much more than a couple of minutes, perhaps even less, but the storm had advanced considerably in that time. Even in my downcast state I became aware of the impending threat as its portentous shadow engulfed us while we hurried along.

When it started, the rain turned rapidly into an unrelenting, heavy downpour. It caught us in the residential backstreets, away from all our normal places of shelter and we were quickly soaked through. Mullet and I traipsed along behind a disconsolately stooping Jake, our heads hung low, sheltering our nostrils as best we could from the worst of the deluge. We walked for a couple of miles without stopping, not even hesitating, the treasures of the restaurant kitchens insufficient temptation to slow down our traverse of the centre. I belatedly sensed where Jake was headed and gave a self-congratulatory tailwag as St. Peter’s steeple came into view through the pall of incessant rain. Its silhouetted form, in the gloom of the tempest-dark early evening, brought a surge of happiness pumping through my veins.

Shelter!

Jake walked past the steps to the church porch and instead headed straight for the presbytery door. We bustled in, dripping water copiously onto the floor of the small entrance vestibule. Mullet and I then expressed our joy at being out of the rain by shaking ourselves vigorously, spraying water liberally up the walls and the front door. Large globules formed quickly, then ran down in rivulets, as if the walls themselves were weeping at the shock of the afternoon's vitriolic viciousness. I watched, transfixed for a second, my mind's eye slowing down real time, imagining the plaster's angst, feeling it squeeze the moisture out of its structure to form yet more tears, tracing the hydration cracks of its anguish.

Father Cuthbert responded quickly to Jake's urgent rap at the door, snapping me out of my trance. I heard him shuffling towards it as soon as Jake had finished knocking. I detected his distinctive smell: his aroma was calm.

"Oh, heaven! You guys are soaking. You'd better come in and dry off."

My senses must have been heightened by the events in the park because as soon as Father Cuthbert had opened the door I noticed that he was enveloped by a faint yellow glow, tinged with pink at the edge. I had never noticed this feature before but it was now quite distinct. Texturally, it wasn't dissimilar to the mist that had shrouded the mob in the park, though it was less turbulent and different in colour. I thought that Jake might say something about it but he either didn't see it or pretended it wasn't there.

"Thank you Father, that's very kind. We got caught up in that colossal storm, far from shelter, and had trust in your kindness. Do you have some towels so that I can dry the worst of the rain off these mutts before we come in?"

"Yes, that's probably a good idea. Hold on, then, I'll go and fetch some from the airing cupboard."

Jake removed his rucksack and took off his saturated overcoat, hanging it up on a hook. The rain had penetrated the coat and his inner clothes had become sodden. He looked cold and tired, his aura faint.

His aura!

I'd not seen it before but, like Father Cuthbert, Jake exuded a faint pinky yellow hue. I turned to look at Mullet and she too had the same aura, fine and wispy, clinging to her like the morning mist caressing the land. Had these auras appeared suddenly, or was it that I was only now becoming aware of them? It most probably was just me because it was very unlikely that the youths in the park had suddenly sprouted red mist. I checked my paws and belly, as much of me as I could, but I couldn't see any of the haze attached to me.

Don't I have an aura? Would I be able to see it if I had one?

"Stop shuffling around. You're spreading water everywhere. Sit still!" commanded Jake.

"Here we are," said Father Cuthbert, returning with his hands full. "You take one towel, Jake. I'll dry this little fella here. You never did give him a name, did you?"

"Thanks, Father. He's quite happy with 'little fella'."

Mullet and I had a good rubdown. Father Cuthbert was very gentle and the towel soft. He remembered to do the inside of my ear flaps, which was yummy. Then we had another good shake before he led us into his kitchen. It was small but pleasingly warm. He had managed to squeeze a small table up against a wall-mounted radiator. Cutlery, napkins, a pepper pot and salt cellar all suggested that this was where he ate his meals.

"Jake, you're soaked through. I'll lend you some of my clothes, then we'll wash and dry those for you. Blast the Bishop, you'll have to sleep in the church tonight."

"Oh, thank you, Father, that is extremely kind."

"Yes, well, we mustn't make a habit out of it, must we? But you really did get caught this evening. Come with me. I'll give you those dry clothes and then you can get washed and changed in the bathroom. You can tell me what happened afterwards, whilst we have something to eat. The dogs will be all right here for a while, yes?"

"Yes, Father."

"I know it's been a hot day but I'll just flip on the heating to help them dry off."

Mullet and I snuggled up under the table next to the radiator. The storm had abated the sultriness of the afternoon and the added warmth was effective at evaporating the remaining moisture from our hair. I dozed, basking in the satisfying sensation, dreaming of summer days lying in the midday sun, legs gently swaying in the luxurious air, rolling over and over on the freshly mown grass, delighting in a cornucopia of scents, teasing pollen-laden honey bees with outrageous leaps, out-shimmying Mullet through the long grass on the hillside outside the city…

"Whewww… doggy in here!" Father Cuthbert exclaimed loudly when he came back into the room, wrenching us both starkly back from our daydreams. He peeked under the table, reassured himself that we were behaving, then started preparing some supper. Now it was impossible to snooze. I crawled out and sat eagerly close to him, donning my cutest soft-dog look, but to no avail. My paw-in-the-air appeal was usually devastatingly effective, but he seemed coldly immune.

"Sit and wait, there's a good little fella."

The aroma intensified. Mullet joined me in assisting Father Cuthbert with our undivided attention and most potent stare. Drool dribbled freely onto the floor.

“Patience, my friends.”

Jake returned, unfortunately adding the stink of antiseptic soap to the heavenly aroma being produced by our host. “Smells delicious, Father. You have been very kind.”

“It’s only spaghetti with mushrooms, aubergines, tomatoes and some herbs. No meat here but still very tasty. Sit yourself down, it’s nearly ready. I thought the dogs might like it so I’ve made some extra for them.”

Woof!

That evening Mullet and I ate off proper dinner plates.

Yum yum delicious!

Didn’t we just feel so dandy? Oh, you’ve seen through me: I’ll admit that we were both a bit rude and scoffed our portions up before Jake and Father Cuthbert had barely begun, but we did have the decency not to beg for their food. No, we were very good dogs. We lay under the table and dozed lightly, serenaded by their conversation.

“So, Jake, you were going to tell me what happened this afternoon.”

“Ah, yes, Father. Well, the dogs and I had gone to the fair to pick up a bite to eat. We had enjoyed the day and were having a rest before making our way to shelter for the night when we witnessed a mob of blueheads attacking a Tembus family. It was horrific, Father. One of the lads torched the woman’s face.”

Despite my state of satisfied slumber, I distinctly remember being puzzled as to why Jake hadn’t mentioned the mob’s vivid aural mist. It had stood out so brilliantly in the dull light of the approaching storm.

"Oh, yes. I've seen that story come up on the local news feed before you arrived. She's been taken to hospital with terrible burns."

"I'm not surprised. She was in agony, Father. They attacked this family without provocation, shouting the most vile obscenities. 'Die you Tembus whore!' They managed to raise their angry shouts even over her hysterical screaming. They may well have killed her if some bystanders hadn't intervened, but the bastards - sorry, Father - managed to get away."

"They've not been caught yet, according to the reports."

"Anyway, Father, it was gruesome. The whole episode must have been over in about a minute but I was so disturbed that I couldn't have been thinking straight and made the wrong decision when it came to trying to avoid the storm. We were totally exposed when the clouds burst. It was such a torrential downpour that we were all soaked through almost instantaneously. It shouldn't have happened. I'm sorry if I've been presumptuous in knocking at your door."

"Well, you're lucky that I was in, and not on parish business. You wouldn't have been able to dry off in the church porch tonight."

A strong whiff of the spaghetti sauce infiltrated my nostrils and I realised - just before Mullet, ha! - that Father Cuthbert was dangling a tasty morsel under the table for us to feast on. I snatched at it, then felt guilty as Mullet's icy look lanced my conscience.

"No," said Jake. "I'll try not to impose like this again, Father. Jeez, that really was a shocking attack! I cannot comprehend how anyone could perpetrate such a vicious, premeditated attack on another human… well, on any living creature actually."

"There's a lot of hate around at the moment, Jake. A lot of posturing, a lot of taking sides. People are becoming involved in this violence who have no real desire for it, they're just being sucked in by the crowd. It's too tribal."

"It's getting out of control, Father. I know many Tembusi in the city who are very frightened. There'll be thugs in their own community who will seek vengeance. The whole thing could spiral."

"Indeed. I'll pray for love to enter their hearts."

"Love? Why, Father, if you don't mind me asking? Haven't you prayed for that before? Haven't we all?"

There was a noticeable pause, silent other than for the sound of knives pushing the last remnants of spaghetti onto forks.

"Well, yes," said Father Cuthbert eventually. "But one must have faith and pray until one's prayers are answered."

"It seems to me that if God is omnipotent," said Jake, "then it is pointless to pray more than the one time. He's heard you. He's either going to do something about it or not. To keep on pestering Him with the same prayer suggests a lack of faith either in Him or in the whole process. You know? 'He's either not listening to me or He can do nothing about it.' Worse still in this situation: He wants to do nothing about it."

"Well, I see where you're coming from, Jake. Prayer is difficult to understand. I'm not sure I could lay claim to understanding it myself," said Father Cuthbert. Then, chuckling, he added: "Though please don't tell my congregation that."

There was another brief silence whilst Father Cuthbert's plate, still with plenty of the sauce splattered on it, was lowered carefully under the table. Still feeling guilty from before, I allowed Mullet to begin licking the plate clean, before assiduously helping her finish off and giving it a good polish.

Father Cuthbert continued: "I often think that prayer is more to do with shaping one's own mind and intent than it is with persuading God to take some specific action. When I pray, I try to clear my mind, I envision good things, try to picture the desired outcome. If everyone could do this, focus their thoughts on the good, then things would inevitably improve, I'm sure of that. And it would seem as if the prayer had been answered."

"So: everyone should meditate, Father."

"Well, that would be a very good beginning but I don't think it's only that. Everyone has to focus on what is good, on love, on the deliverance from suffering. That is why it is important that we should all pray for love to enter their hearts - and all of our hearts. Today, tomorrow and always. It is important to keep praying. To keep myself in the right frame of mind, but also in the hope that others will be inspired by my actions to do likewise. Then the world will change for the better."

"And where does God fit into all of this?" asked Jake.

Father Cuthbert was silent awhile, then muttered almost inaudibly: "Jake, it was you who mentioned God, not I."

15 THE STREET

The street lay quiet and peaceful in the crisp winter night. Stars twinkled in the infinite sky, sharp and clear now that the streetlights had been snuffed out by their midnight curfew.

Wind: there was none.

The dust lay still.

Light spilling from warm windows: none.

Although darkness ruled, ancient eyes, used to seeing in the darkest of Dark Age winter nights, were able to penetrate the deception of gloom.

Ha! Not so clever, are they? All these cars, always criss-crossing back and forth at all times of day and night: don't they realise that their headlamps, reflected off this wonderful city's buildings, here and there, up and down, reveal the blackest night's secrets to me? Maybe they're on my side. I can see it all, and now that I've recognised the subversive invasion afoot, I will not cease my surveillance. There's verve in these old holy stones yet.

Oh, and what joy continuous surveillance can bring! The blueheads are gaining momentum all over the city. That march over a year ago, in this very street, started it all off. And now they are spreading all over the city. Brave citizen soldiers parading, shouting and yelling for the darky Tembusi to go back to their homelands.

Hurrah! The crusadic spirit lives on.

It appears that there are sufficient brave souls willing to battle for Christian values. Have you seen them attack the houses of the infidel? Have you seen them hurl stones and bricks? It warms my tabernacle to the core.

They would do more, much more, had it not been for the spols. But I can't blame the spols: they did allow the blueheads some leeway. It would probably be too much at this stage to allow the firebombing of Tembusi houses. Let's not forget that we want to reclaim them for proper citizens once they have been ousted. So, no, mustn't blame them.

The Tembusi are seeing the determination of proper, true crusaders to evict them from our civilized city. It can only be a matter of time before they all pack up and go. Then the street will repopulate with good Christian minded people and I can begin to regain my influence on the city.

But....

What's this? Who is that approaching the presbytery? All dressed in black garb? That looks like a Tembus. How can this be? He's entered the porch. What? Has Father Cuthbert invited him in?

Unbelievable!

16 A VISIT

It was not surprising that St. Peter had failed to notice the Kudnok until the dim light emanating from the presbytery porch revealed his presence. The Kudnok had dressed carefully for the occasion, not wishing to elicit any attention. An immigrant from the south, he had dressed in darkest black, from the cap on his head to the shoes on his feet. He was, effectively, invisible in the city night.

Conscious of the revelatory nature of the lamp that Father Cuthbert always left on in the porch as a welcome to visitors, whatever time of night they might seek spiritual support, he turned in quickly, lowering his head into his chest so as to shield his face from any prying eyes, and rang the doorbell. He had come unannounced at a late hour and so was surprised when, almost immediately, he heard the clang of an internal door opening and closing, then footsteps approaching.

Father Cuthbert opened the door wide, confidently, clearly not fearing burglars or assailants, but his expression betrayed surprise when he faced his visitor:

"Kudnok Abdul! My! What brings you here at this hour? Come in, come in."

"Thank you, Father. I've come to speak with you, if I may, about matters affecting both our communities."

“Surely, Kudnok, but why so late and unannounced?” Father Cuthbert led the Kudnok through to his welcoming kitchen. “I was about to get ready for bed. Would you like some tea?”

“Please, Father,” said the Kudnok. “I apologise for the late hour. I did not want to be seen entering your home. I would rather discuss what I need in private and gauge your reaction. The time for any public appearances will come later, depending on your feedback.”

“Well, I have to say you’re making it sound very covert. All very exciting. I’m only a simple man of the cloth, you know. But, anyway, I trust you are well and that the life of your kroda is healthy. Sugar? Milk?”

“Please, Father.” Kudnok Abdul sat at the small table, watching Father Cuthbert quietly for a short moment. They had met briefly at a civic gathering some months ago and exchanged pleasantries. Each had left with a favourable impression of the other, but this was the first time that they had been alone, able to speak as they might wish without being overheard, and without the constant interruption of others.

“Well, yes, I am well, but there is much anxiety within my community, Father. Recent developments - specifically, the mutilation of the Tembus mother at the fair and the continuing processions of the blueheads through our streets - have caused deep concern. Everyone is frightened. Many people are angry.”

“Understandable, certainly. Totally deplorable actions. I have condemned them unequivocally in my sermons.”

“So I have heard, Father.”

“Oh?” said Father Cuthbert, serving the tea, which he had brewed in the drinking mug, too tired to cerimonialise with the pot. He sat opposite the Kudnok and gave a wry smile: "You're very well informed."

"Your reputation travels far, Father."

"My reputation?"

"Yes, as a man of compassion, as a liberal, as a spiritual person."

"A spiritual person?" Father Cuthbert paused, musing. "I'm not sure what you mean, Kudnok. I'm a Catholic priest."

"Of course. What I mean is that you have a reputation for seeing beyond pure dogma. You refuse to be a strict adherent to the whims of Church politics. You have the ability to take a holistic view of the world. Am I right?"

"Well, I suppose so, but what of it? Am I that different to other priests? Take a biscuit, please, Kudnok. These are rather tasty."

The Kudnok scrunched his face up, shrugged slightly, took a nibble.

"Is that why you've come to see me?" asked Father Cuthbert.

"The fabric of our city is in danger of melting with racial hatred. The bluehead marches are fuelling resentment in both of our communities. If it goes unchecked, the hatred and violence will spiral. We need to do something to help vulnerable people who could easily be manipulated by agitators on either side. You, Father, as a spiritual leader of a significant faith in the city, have a major role to play."

The Kudnok paused briefly, letting the weight of his challenge take effect. "But your action would be much more effective if you were to take it in concert with ourselves; if you involved the Tembus community in your initiative."

Father Cuthbert's response was brusque, perhaps too sudden and unthinking: "I don't see how we could act together in this, Kudnok.

Our respective communities are so different. I will lead a prayer for peace between our communities at Sunday mass."

"A prayer? Father! What good will that do?"

The Kudnok appeared to be agitated.

"What do you mean, Kudnok? Don't you believe in God? Surely you believe in the power of prayer?"

"Of course I do, Father, but primarily as a means of affecting the minds of individuals, not as a process for bringing about change in the community beyond your immediate churchgoers. We need something more direct, more worldly."

"Kudnok, if you don't mind me saying, you seem to have some unorthodox views."

"Pah! Unorthodox? We are all unorthodox! Where is the orthodox view in my religion? Many people have their own interpretations of the Holy Books. Different factions have been murdering each other for centuries. It's the same in your religion, Father. Protestants and Catholics? Don't get me started! Same in every other religion on the planet. I'm not an idol worshipper! Bloodshed. Bloodshed! Millions and millions of gallons of blood, all down the ages. Guts, brains and all. Bloodshed! If that's what orthodoxy brings, Father, you can bury it deep, deep underground and forget about it!"

The Kudnok was apoplectic. Spittle showered Father Cuthbert and he drew himself back in his chair, protecting his face with his hands.

Taking a deep, calming breath, the Kudnok continued: "You misunderstand me, Father. Of course I believe in prayer. Of course I believe in God. But who is God, my dear Father? Your God is the same as my God. The Tefors were ascetic meditators who spent long periods in the wilderness finding the truth. The truth within themselves. Their truths - God's revelations - are, in their fundamental elements, the same. Any differences are surely the result of Man's distortion down the ages, both on your side and ours. So why are our two communities at loggerheads, Father? We are the same people of God. I ask you, Father…"

Father Cuthbert sat still, finishing his last biscuit, looking at the Kudnok, but offered no reply. The Kudnok had said enough. He glared at the priest, pressurising him to reply.

Father Cuthbert wasn't ready, but felt compelled to break his silence: "Well, your Tefor condoned violence, unlike Jesus, who condemned it."

The Kudnok splurted violently, splattering the table in tea droplets and biscuit crumbs. Father Cuthbert ventured to dab at the mess with a tea towel, despite the Kudnok launching another tirade:

"I cannot believe you have just said that, Father. Why then did Jesus go around with a band of armed men? Eh? Answer me that! The apostles had swords! And they used them! What was that business when He was arrested? And the temple? Throw everyone out of their market without threatening them with force? Get real, Father! He yielded a whip to drive them out. With His sword swinging cronies behind Him. It's hardly a holy morality to go around preaching peace and love when you have twelve armed men standing alongside. And Christianity is responsible for some of the bloodiest crimes in history. Genocides galore. Be serious, please! This issue is not about religion. It's about people. Yours and mine. People!"

The Kudnok slammed the table with his fist. Father Cuthbert was stunned. He opened his mouth to respond but thought better of it. The Kudnok continued: "Jesus and the Tefor were both men of their time. They lived when they lived, where they lived. Both would have found it impossible not to be touched by violence at some stage of their lives.

But both were men of peace. Anyone with any sense – and I'm sure that includes you, Father - knows that the Tefor was a man of peace."

Father Cuthbert was glad of the Kudnok's attempt at appeasement, using it as an opportunity to reengage: "But you have many in your community who profess that violence is the only way to counter the rabidity of the blueheads. I can't support violence in any form, Kudnok."

"Precisely, Father, precisely. Neither can I. And, yes, we have those people in our community, as you do in yours. There are people who spit at Tembusi, even here in the street. There are those who vandalise our krodas; those who would kill Tembusi. The reality is that even the most placid will defend their families and their homes if sufficiently provoked. So, yes, we have hotheads. But, Father, it is precisely for that reason that you and I must act now to diffuse the tension, to harmonise the noise debilitating our communities.

"There are many vulnerable people in our city who are ripe for harvesting by the blueheads and other agitators. Others will just follow meekly: keen to be part of the gang; part of the clan; part of the tribe. Others still will want to be seen to move up a place in the queue. Vying for visibility they fall into the pit dug by those who get their kicks from violence.

"But we are all the same! You and I must make the vulnerable minds in our communities - the bulk – believe in that. We have to offer them an alternative! Love, understanding, tolerance. We must, or we surrender to the cauldron that will soon explode. Your job – and mine – should be to voice the sound of reason, of compassion, of the equality of man and of religion. Your job and mine, dear Father, is to foster unity between men and religion in our troubled city."

The Kudnok barely paused for breath before continuing: "We are born. We choose not the place nor the time. We are conditioned by the circumstances of our parents' upbringing and the locality we arrive at in this world. That city - Tembus. This city - Christian. From that point on, it's every man or woman for themselves. Life is a big struggle, Father. For those of us who are – fortunately or unfortunately – born with the capacity to think and philosophise, there is then a lot of unravelling to do. God? Father, have you looked into the depths of the oceans? Have you looked at the night sky? Father? Have you seen the stars, the constellations, the galaxies?"

The Kudnok paused again, this time clearly for dramatic effect, because he resumed before Father Cuthbert could answer: "Tell me that we - any of us - either you, the Catholics, or us, the Tembusi, or even other faiths perhaps, are the 'chosen ones'. Or is that just the understandable belief of people from many centuries ago, living in pockets of isolated population, when meeting a Tefor? Father? Tell me honestly."

Again, the Kudnok offered no chance of a riposte from Father Cuthbert, should he have wanted to offer one. "God, in all this unimaginably vast world with its myriad of life forms, let alone what else might be out there in the immensity of the universe, is looking down on each one of us individually, constantly, each one of us eight and a half billion, to see if we worship him daily, his angels monitoring our every move and thought. Father?"

This time Father Cuthbert was ready with a reply: "But surely that is the basis of our faith. Faith, Kudnok. My faith in the all supreme Christian God and you, your faith in yours."

"But He is the same God, my dear Father. There is only one God. One! Different peoples born in different parts of the world at different times call Him by a different name."

Silence becalmed them then, as if heaven itself had draped a soft velvet cloth over the scene, enfolding them in its embrace.

Gently, the Kudnok ventured to speak again: "Father, you and I are no different in our roles as religious leaders. Our flocks are looking for guidance to help them survive the turmoil of their daily lives; to help them make the world sufferable. That is what we are here for, to ease their passage through the confusion of life."

"But what about Truth?"

"Will we ever know it, Father? The Buddhists have it right: they do not bother to ask why, or who, or what because they know that these questions are impossible to answer. I simply try to explain the most harmonious way of life to people."

The Kudnok's teasing had finally prompted Father Cuthbert to ask the crucial question; its utterance in itself a signal of acquiescence: "What did you have in mind for me to do, Kudnok? Why me?"

"Surely you can see, Father. You are a pillar of the Christian community. Be seen with us. Be seen with the Tembus community. Show that you welcome our integration. Come to some of the events at our kroda, perhaps bring some of your flock."

"The Bishop won't approve. He's very conservative."

"The Bishop, the Bishop! Father, you know in your heart that you can only be true to yourself. That, my dear Father, is the real truth you seek."

Father Cuthbert was silent but this time the Kudnok did not resume talking, forcing the priest to speak: "I'll think on it. Thank you for your visit, Kudnok."

With that, the Kudnok stood up and walked towards the door. Father Cuthbert overtook him softly, then kindly opened the door to the porch for the Kudnok.

"May God bless you. Follow your heart, Father"

The pair embraced warmly, then the Kudnok stepped out and was absorbed by the night.

"Farewell, Kudnok, farewell," called out Father Cuthbert in a whisper. "I have enjoyed your visit."

Turning the corner with Father Cuthbert's friendly send-off still warming his heart, the Kudnok heard a lifeless, creepy, shimmering tinkle shearing the night's silence, like shards of glass shrapnel piercing soft skin.

St. Peter's bells! What is Father Cuthbert doing tinkering with the bells at this deep hour of the night? He really is a most extraordinary fellow.

In their beds, the long suffering residents of the street once more had to take refuge under their pillows and duvets, terrified by the unearthly sounds of St. Peter's.

Of all the people in the street, Father Cuthbert was the only one not to hear the bellicose wail. After the Kudnok had left, he had rushed to his bedroom, knelt into his meditation pose, inhaled deeply, emptied his mind with the exhalation, then focused on his normal breath, entering the calm of the universe. And there he stayed, resonating, until dawn's first light triggered his return to the mundane world of the street.

17 NOT FROM HERE

Anxiety had blighted the city in the aftermath of the bluehead marches and attacks. It had even affected the University, although to a much lesser extent. Here one could still find people with broad views with whom one could converse and feel the resonant warmth of shared feeling.

The violent events in the city had polarised opinion. Neither side was telling the truth. Objective thought had been severely wounded, mirroring the physical victims. In the street, youths had coalesced into vigilante groups, threatening any non-residents, jostling them away. Bluehead gangs roamed throughout the city. There would often be a stand-off in the vicinity of the street, which the spols tried to prevent escalating into fighting, mostly successfully. In response, we had adapted our routine and altered our route through the city into the University. No more short-cuts: we knew the safe routes and rarely ventured off them.

People across the country were complaining of a lack of protection from the spols against the blueheads; of collusion in attacks on krodas and of strategic withdrawals prior to the pillaging of streets such as ours. These injustices led to the formation of a peaceful protest movement whose objective was to promote multi-cultural understanding. This Cause had the support not only of the population that felt under the most threat, but also of many liberals who saw through the xenophobic propaganda. It was popular and many students at the University - of all ethnicities and religions - supported it.

Seth was a keen adherent. He brought propaganda home from the Students' Union, plastered his bedroom and the communal kitchen with promotional posters, and was keen to talk about its policies and strategies. One evening he took me along to an event that the Cause had organised. The speaker projected a video from his 'Pulse. He claimed that it had been removed from the net by the spols and that the Cause had the only copies. The programme shocked. It depicted scenes of nausea-inducing inhumanity perpetrated by blueheads on victims across the country. I was reminded of the scenes in the street just after I'd moved in, of the horror on the little girl's face. Watching the video was like living my dreams.

"Well, that was pretty horrific," said Seth as we were leaving the cuboid union building.

"Yep. Shocking. Absolutely. What a mess."

We walked on a few hundred yards in silence, hands buried deep in pockets, heads bowed. Eventually, Seth mumbled: "I don't know how we get out of this jam."

"No, nor me. We seem to be ingrained in this cycle of hate and depravity."

"It's institutionalised, man. That has to stop. It's being instigated by Government. The people just pick up on it because it's what they're being spoon-fed. Have to stop that, we have to stop that."

"Easier said than done. It's an elected Government. The people must support it."

"Nah, not really, they're simply falling in behind what the media tells them to believe. It's the media, man, they're the ones pulling the strings, controlling the Government, man. They're in charge, them guys and the businesses behind them."

"We're schtuk then, I don't know how we move."

Despite our recent caution, we had been distracted on our way home. Our minds dwelt on the video we had just seen and our conversation was intense. Falling back on older habits, we had slipped into a dark side-street, a short-cut bypassing two better-lit sides of a triangle. Looking up, I could make out three people walking towards us, a few yards ahead. They walked slowly side by side, blocking the pavement. Parked cars lined the road. We would be blocked in. I sensed they were not going to let us pass.

"We'd better turn round, Seth, quick! Let's go the long way."

I turned and upped my pace, but Seth had been shoegazing, deep in thought. Rather than turn and run, he looked up to assess the situation. Fatal mistake. Without him behind me, I hesitated. They were on us almost instantly and, with a crunch, pinned us both against a parked estate. I felt a jab of piercing pain in my groin and then my head was tugged back as the thug twisted me around and caught me in a head lock. One arm was wrenched up viciously. The pain and lack of air rendered my free arm useless. It wouldn't have made any difference: my years of experience in the playground had taught me that offering a fight would be asking for trouble. Wait, see how this panned out, that was my instinct.

The thug spun me round again, loosening his grip slightly so that I could see Seth. The other two still had him pinned against the car and were giving him a beating. Blood poured from his nose and mouth. Seth moaned as another punch landed on his belly.

"You fucking Tembus cunt. What the fuck you doing in our city? Fucking Tembus bastard!"

And he spat on Seth, full in the face. That was the biggest thug, the one landing the most blows, clearly the 'moral' inspiration for the other two. He continued shouting insults. At least when he was doing that he stopped the beating. When Seth was nearly unconscious, the thug made sure his crony held him securely against the car before turning his attention to me:

"And you, what you doing fraternising with this cunt? Call yourself a white boy? Come to think of it, you look a bit dark yourself." He jabbed me between the eyes with a steely finger. "You a Tembus too?"

"No," I stuttered, feeling ashamed, even if it was the truth.

"No? No? Then what you doing with this filth? You fraternise with them, boy, and you're made from the same shit. What you doing here, hey? Where do you come from? You're not from the city."

Violently, he grabbed my face, squeezing hard between the cheeks, then slammed me into the car.

"You boys don't belong in this city. Now, let's reinforce that important lesson."

I steeled myself for the beating to resume, wincing before the first blow fell.

"Oi! Get off my car!" a man shouted, stepping forward from the door of a nearby house, straight out onto the pavement. He was holding a baseball bat.

"That's my car. Get off those guys, let them go."

"They're Tembus cunts, they shouldn't be here, we're just teaching them a lesson," said the leading thug.

Two more men stepped out of the house, also yielding baseball bats. They were younger than the first man, his sons perhaps, but old enough and sufficiently physically commanding to impose a presence. The three of them stood abreast: another impassable barrier.

"Git!" shouted the first man.

"Alright, alright, mister, but I'd watch your step in future if I was you. You're a marked man!" Said with menace. He motioned to his cronies, who slowly released us from our holds and stepped back alongside their leader, facing the baseball bat yielding trio. They turned, slowly, then swaggered off from whence they had come, never once looking round.

The baseballers remained immobile, impassive, focussed on the growing distance to the thugs. Seth and I mirrored them, frozen by the unvoiced command of our saviours. When the thugs were barely visible in the gloom, the older man relaxed, turned to us and shouted:

"Now git! Never darken this way again." And, with venom: "Git!"

We responded without hesitation, moving back towards the main, brightly lit avenue as fast as we could. Seth was limping badly; he'd taken some heavy kicks to his shins, as well as his groin area and he was struggling to see. One eye had already closed up from the blows, and the other was heavily swollen. I guided him home, arm round his shoulders. He leant on me as much as he could without slowing me down too much.

♦ ♦ ♦

That night, alone in my room, I sat in the dark. No point trying to go to sleep. The images of the blows landing sickeningly on Seth burned in my mind. But worse was to come as the images shifted to my own inability to help my friend, either physically or morally.

"You a Tembus too?" the thug had asked.

"No," I had blurted.

Of course, I wasn't a Tembus, but that's not the point. The point was that, at that moment, I had no thoughts for Seth, no concern about how to help him, either with deeds or words. I cared only for myself. A nauseating weakling, hoping only to minimise my own pain. I would have said anything that I thought might have dissuaded the thugs from harming me, even if it was at Seth's expense.

"You a Tembus too?" the thug asked.

"No."

"No."

"No."

Coward.

Coward!

My mind span. I vomited onto the carpet, smearing my trousers and shoes, then fell off the bed onto my knees, folded onto the floor, and sobbed.

18 THE STREET

St. Peter was chuffed. At last, Father Cuthbert had done something good and positive. St. Peter was seeing the evidence himself. And today, on this holiest of holy days: Easter Sunday. What a joy to see such a sizeable number of people flocking to the church to worship God. St. Peter was sure that this was the largest congregation for many years, decades even. He allowed himself a moment's daydream, envisioning people, the old as well as the young, having to stand at the back and in the aisles, the pews bursting with souls ready for cleansing.

Father Cuthbert must have somehow succeeded in spreading the good news of Christ far and wide, well beyond the street. Many worshippers had come in their cars, the lucky ones parking them up on the pavement like the residents of the street, the others having to find slots in and off the avenue close by and walk. St. Peter observed with pleasure that some were even jogging hurriedly to ensure that they were in time for the service.

Now that everyone was inside the church, quiet reigned in the street once again. St. Peter concentrated on focussing his stones to listen to Father Cuthbert preach on this momentous occasion. How would he welcome this magnificent congregation? How would he react? If he harnessed this resurgent energy effectively then this could turn out to be a significant moment for St. Peter: the start of the revitalisation of the Church and the pushback of the infidel.

And so he bedded himself down onto his foundations, lightening the weight of many years and listened. Yes, it was working. The design of the church was perfect in this way: when he focussed he could hear every word coming from the altar. There was nothing special at first. The opening welcome was brief and Father Cuthbert made no mention of the unusual size of the congregation.

Is the fool going to waste this opportunity?

Odd: Father Cuthbert then moved straight into the standard service.

The special address will come during the homily then, it must do.

St. Peter relaxed, letting the priest's words soothe him. He could tell how the acoustic of the building had changed with the throng. The tone was soft and warm. It reminded him of the halcyon days of centuries past when such occasions were common and not even reserved for special holy days.

Then, a subtle change in the acoustic troubled him. There was a hubbub coming from immediately outside of the church. He quickly switched the focus of his attention to the street. What he saw alarmed him to his chalice.

Heresy!

There, not more than twenty yards away up the street were thirty or forty people, chanting in a strange language. They were heading towards the front entrance of the church. And there, leading them, was that not the dastardly kudnok who had spent time with Father Cuthbert? By Galadriel, yes it was. What was this new affront?

What?

They have reached the entrance, and the door has been opened mid-service.

There's a gesture of welcome from within. They are entering.

Curses!

St. Peter's bells rang out in fury but, on this occasion, all who heard interpreted only the sound of a joyful celebration.

19 EASTER SUNDAY

The reader finished the gospel extract. This was the moment. Father Cuthbert walked slowly to the pulpit and began his homily, eyeing the congregation with the confidence of a man knowing that he is following his soul.

"What a welcome influx of people on this Easter Sunday. Welcome, and may the love of God be with you all. Hopefully those of you standing are not too uncomfortable. An especial welcome indeed to our Tembus brothers and sisters who have walked over from the City Kroda in our neighbourhood. There must be many tens of our brothers and sisters who have made the trip today. Correct, Kudnok?

"We're very thankful for this beautiful visit. It's an expression of the love and compassion that bind us with the City Kroda. It's a love and compassion that are helping to bring our two communities closer as one, especially during recent months, when we have each helped each other during the disturbances in the city, sharing first aid and shelter. That was very beautiful.

"We have become true friends, not just neighbours. The neighbour relationship between us is being transformed into a profound human relationship filled with compassion and love, and a lot of beauty. Would you like to say something, Kudnok? Please go ahead."

Scattered applause rang out, rising as Father Cuthbert stepped aside, gesturing for the Kudnok, who was standing in the crowded aisle, to come to the pulpit. The Kudnok came forward central to the altar, bowed, then stepped forward slowly as the applause grew to an ovation.

“In the name of God, the most Gracious, the most Merciful. First of all, I am your brother, the Kudnok and speaker of the City Kroda. I have conducted my doctoral studies at the university in Holy Book rhetoric.

“In recent times, we at the City Kroda have been building strong intimate ties with your own Church. Ours is a relationship of love and of friendship: an all-citizen relationship at its base.”

As if this was a prompt, the visitors from the City Kroda called out in one, strong voice:

“United, like one hand. Long live the kranul, side by side with the cross.”

Kudnok Abdul smiled, then continued, his voice as confident as Father Cuthbert’s had been before him.

“In the name of God, the most Gracious, the most Merciful. I believe that the type of relationship that binds me with St. Peter’s Church is one that has been dictated upon me by Lajat, because Lajat instructs us to be kind to our neighbours. It is therefore a relationship that draws from two traditions: the spirit of our faith and the spirit of our shared city.

“This city, on whose land both Tembusi and Christians have spilled of their blood in the recent troubles, cannot thrive unless all of its citizens remain united as one hand, without the slightest difference between them.

“It is in this city that the great Fadil Pasha - a Catholic - lived, and that the eminent Richard Evans - a Tembus - lived. It is here that many other noteworthy people were born and lived: Tembus, Catholic and of other faiths. All enriched this city together. Their religion may have helped develop them into the people that they were but their religion never made them less worthy, less significant or less important than any others.

"This is a great city, through which our famous river flows since the beginning of creation, and from which drink all those who tread these streets, irrespective of creed or sect. Those who think that the pillars of this city are supported by only one faith are most certainly wrong. Because the pillars of this city are the result of the toil and sweat of all its citizens. By the hands of all its citizens: Catholics, Tembusi and others.

"This Church - St. Peter's - has taken on a special significance during the recent troubles. It has opened its doors to those in need of shelter, to anyone caught up in the disturbances, just as the City Kroda opened its doors to anyone, irrespective of name, or creed, or colour. Because this city, through all of the tough times that it has traversed, has embraced all of its people, and has risen with the hands of its children. This great city will remain a safe place to live, by the will of God, safeguarded by those who tread her streets: Tembusi, Catholics and others."

Again the visitors applauded and called out:

"United, like one hand. Long live the kranul, side by side with the cross."

This time they were joined by many of the Catholics in the congregation.

"Our march today from the City Kroda to St. Peter's Church is a message that I direct to the enemies of humanity, both from outside the city and within. Just as the people of this city have stood united as one hand during the recent troubles, then so we will remain, by the will of God, strong, defiant and dignified, with the hearts of its people confident that they will lead this city to the shores of safety, even if our wait for this day prolongs.

“This city and its citizens are capable of solving her own problems. This city will solve its religious problems, solve its sectarian problems. This city’s problems are in the mind only. The problem of this city is a problem of mentality. We need to understand and revive the spirit of this city, the spirit of Lajat, the spirit of Christianity, the spirit of brotherhood between peoples in a new way. We want to dialogue and converse with each other. We need to cooperate and collaborate where we agree, and dialogue among ourselves where we disagree. We want this city to remain, through its citizens, a strong and productive community.

“You would not find a single workplace in this city where the workers are all Tembus, or are all Christian. Not a single one. Indeed, you might not be able to distinguish between the Tembusi and the Christians. You might not be able to find a neighbourhood where Tembusi do not live alongside their Christian brethren. Here in this city, there are people whose fathers are Tembusi, and whose mothers are Catholics. And in the recent troubles, many of us stood beside the other, and no one asked the other about his name, his political orientation or his religion. Humanity prevailed and each helped the other, irrespective of trifles.”

The Kudnok paused, more for effect than for breath, surveying his rapt audience. The church was silent, hanging on his next words.

“Dozens of people have come with me to St. Peter’s Church today, thousands more in spirit. They have all come to you, to offer their well-wishes and greetings. Their sincere well-wishes and greetings. To you, on your special holy day.”

Warm applause broke out amongst the congregation, taking a long time to subside. Eventually, the Kudnok held up his hands, moving them gently from side to side, as if asking to be allowed to finish. The previous dust defying silence resumed.

"This city will remain strong because of you: her discerning children. And let us together prevent the vandals that may take advantage of this sensitive period from destroying our city."

And, finally, with emphasis:

"This city will remain safe and tranquil because of you. United like one hand."

And the congregation responded in unison: "United like one hand!" and then broke into thunderous applause.

Father Cuthbert, who had stood motionless by the side of the altar during the Kudnok's address, now approached and embraced him, tears of emotion running down his cheeks.

The Kudnok stepped forward from the pulpit, spread out his arms, palms outstretched, then brought them back together and into his chest, in a gesture of thanks. The applause subsided.

"I thank you for giving me the opportunity to speak and may God bless you all."

The Kudnok returned to his standing position in the aisle. Father Cuthbert chose not to add anything to the Kudnok's address, instead carrying speedily on with the order of the mass. At the offering of peace the Tembus visitors were warmly greeted with handshakes and embraces and, during communion, all approached the altar to be blessed by Father Cuthbert.

Before moving on to the concluding rite, Father Cuthbert made an announcement:

"For those who are able to come after this mass, at Kudnok Abdul's kind invitation, we will walk in procession to the City Kroda, where our kind neighbours have laid on some refreshments. All are welcome. Thank you Kudnok, thank you."

The mass was soon over. Father Cuthbert walked down the aisle, shook the Kudnok's hand once more, then the pair of them moved on out of the Church alongside each other, followed by pairings of parishioners and visitors together until no more were left. Some hundred or more parishioners brought up the rear of the procession towards the City Kroda. It was an impressive sight. It brought a cheer to everyone watching from their houses as they marched down the middle of the street, singing and chanting. The bells of St. Peter tolled joyously, encouraging them on their way.

Joyously?

How wrong could the marchers and the bystanders be? St. Peter, that rock which bore the weight of the whole Christian church, was apoplectic, his bells ringing with furious displeasure.

A kudnok! Addressing *his* parishioners – those whose souls had been entrusted to *him*, belonged to *his* God, not some impostor.

Father Cuthbert has betrayed his Christ, he thought. *He will burn in hell for this!*

♦ ♦ ♦

Sitting alone in the empty church, Mrs. Smith wiped the moisture from her cheeks. Many emotional tears had been shed that day but hers were tears of grief, not of joy. She, and she alone, because she shared it, detected the anger in the peals of St. Peter.

There, in that moment still fresh with the perfume of joy and love, she determined that something must be done about the treacherous Father Cuthbert.

20 A DEMONSTRATION

We were up and away before the birds on the day of the demonstration in the capital. The Students' Union had organised the fleet of buses to transport all the activists on the two hour journey.

Seth and I had signed up a couple of weeks before, as soon as the trip had been announced. I had clearly underestimated the level of support for the Cause within the student community. It was only on turning the corner into the tree-lined avenue that the Union building fronted that I grasped the enormity of the conviction. The sun had not yet risen but the street lights reflected off the bodies of a long line of buses that stretched from the corner, well beyond the Union building itself and as far as the eye could see towards the centre. There must have been thirty buses or more. The fine hairs on the nape of my neck stood erect, a wave of emotion coursing my body. After weeks of despair this very evident sign that my views of the current situation were shared by many reignited my life force. Suddenly, I felt elated.

"Wow!" said Seth.

Wow!

I was awestruck at the sight but said nothing as I tried to forge a new comprehension of the situation in my mind. How could circumstances have got so far out of hand, when there was this much support for tolerance towards all communities?

We joined the line of students snaking through the check-in system to be allocated a bus, revelling in the babble of excited voices.

It took half an hour, getting cold in the pre-dawn, only the brightest of stars managing to adorn the lightening sky, outshining the twilight.

The bus was cosy and I snuggled into my seat, knees tucked high into my body and my hoodie up to maximise the warming effect. Other students were still boarding, shuffling past in the aisle, creating a gentle vibration of movement and sound. It acted like a lullaby, causing the tiredness of previous months to catch up with me. Released from the purgatory of dejection by the elation at seeing the tangible support for the Cause, my body relaxed and fell into a deep sleep. I did not witness our departure, waking slowly only when we were travelling at speed on the motorway. I stayed silent and still, allowing myself to wallow in the luxury of the peace that had touched me. The rest of the bus was quiet too. Seth still slept, as did those others I could see without moving from my seat. I revelled in the feeling of being close to so many others who shared my thoughts: perhaps I was not isolated in the world after all.

We soon arrived at the outskirts of the capital. The road narrowed, the traffic increased and the buildings towered up around us. First came monolithic office buildings, some functional, others flamboyant, heralding the wealth of ambition of their shareholders; then, as we entered the capital proper, high-rise apartments displaced the ostentatious displays of commerce. Finally, as we approached the centre the buildings aged, had more elegance. Progress slowed to a crawl as we made our way towards the river in a procession of buses. The pavements were already thronging with demonstrators, not just students but people of all ages, many carrying banners, and already chanting slogans.

"We are.

All the same!

We are all the same!"

"One world. One city. One people!"

"What do we want?"

"Peace!"

"When do we want it?"

"Now!"

It was an awe inspiring sight.

Eventually we parked alongside the river and everyone on the bus stood up, impatient to clamber out onto the embankment and ease the aches from their legs and backs. I peered out of the window, drinking in the excitement of the crowd, eager to join the throng. We'd clearly been in convoy all the way from the city and had parked in line: I could recognise students that had been in the queue ahead of us and had already alighted.

And there!

There!

Mimi!

Mimi was on the march!

I could not miss this opportunity. Everything else vanished from my thoughts. Mimi became my world. In my urgency to get off the bus, I bolted past Seth into the aisle with a rushed "I'll see you later." Then I barged inelegantly through to the front in my determination to catch up with her, treading on toes that did not make way and excusing myself as best I could. I didn't care who I hurt; the overriding imperative was to be off that bus and in pursuit of Mimi. I spilt onto the pavement, falling on the ground, but bounced back up like a rubber toy and weaved my way in the direction I'd last seen her.

"Mimi. Mimi!" I called shamelessly.

Without the advantage of the bus's height, I had lost sight of her. Panic started to strangulate my voice, bile rising from my stomach, burning my vocal chords. The only way to make headway was to use people in the tightly packed throng to bounce off, then rush forward into the space left by their deflection. I did this repeatedly without pausing, ignoring the invective curses aimed in my direction, still calling out for the focus of my thoughts.

"Mimi! Mimi!"

Then, as despair threatened to squash me underfoot, I heard her return my call:

"Michael. Michael! Over here."

I still couldn't see her through the mass of bodies but the magical sound was all I needed to pinball my way closer.

And there she was! When we met she threw her arms round my neck and planted a kiss on my cheek. I experienced an emotional orgasm the like of which I'd never felt before. It was like a tidal wave had suddenly materialised inside my body and, finding no means of escape, swept through from hair to toe, crashing off the extremities, bouncing back and colliding with itself, causing recurring tremors of excitement that shook me physically. My cock was harder than I'd ever known, as if a steel girder had spontaneously sprouted from my groin.

"Michael! Isn't this fantastic? All these people supporting the Cause. Isn't it great?"

I was clearly not in control of my body at that moment and could not speak but was dimly aware that my facial muscles had been beset into an idiotic grin. Mimi must have taken this as a positive affirmation to her rhetorical question because she turned and followed the flow of the crowd, gesturing me to do likewise. I caught up and we walked side by side, often touching arms from the pressure of the others around us. Despite her kiss and enthusiasm, I still felt too scared to put my arm round her or hold her hand: the scar of that previous rejection, so many years ago now, remained incandescent in my soul.

Eventually I recovered sufficiently to speak:

“I didn’t know you supported the Cause…”

“Of course. Nor me you. Great to see you here though. Isn’t this fantastic?”

“Yeah, it’s great to see so many people actually turn up rather than just twitter.”

“Sure. It makes it real, makes it tangible. It makes those buggers up in Government sit up and take notice.”

“Yeah.”

Banal. I could think of nothing to say. Her proximity muddled my brain. I dared myself to touch her, to hold her hand, but I kept failing the challenge. We drifted with the demo, like flotsam on a river, mimicking the water alongside us. My body was tense from indecision and fear. It felt as if Mimi was pulling me along, like a child with a balloon. I bumbled onward, awash with the tension of the early universe; each cell in my body, each neuron, alive with the maelstrom of primeval elemental force.

Did we follow the demonstration to the square? Did we listen to the speeches? Did we join in with the chanting? Where and what did we eat? Were we surprised at the number of spol drones haranguing the march? But there was no demonstration for me. There was no Cause. All I could think of was Mimi and how to advance our relationship. I yearned to return that touch, that greeting kiss, make it endure and last a lifetime. I knew ours was the perfect match.

But the moment would not come. Just like all those years ago when my mind had been incapable of turning my body into her driveway, even when the compulsion to make a move became irresistible, I was incapable of taking action. After the speeches were over, as we made our way back to the buses, I became increasingly anxious. We walked in silence. I felt as if an unbridgeable chasm separated us. I sank into deep despair.

Arriving back at the embankment the thought of our impending departure broke through the anguish. I recognised that we'd reached a life tipping moment. We would have to split up and return on separate buses. If there was anything to be salvaged between us, then it would have to be done now. Miraculously, it was Mimi who proffered the solution:

"Michael, give me your 'Pulse. Let's keep in touch."

Sweet words!

We exchanged numbers but the lingering fear from those previous rejections held me back from giving her the passionate farewell kiss that I so yearned for. We said a meek goodbye with inoffensive pecks to the cheeks and then I waved as she clambered onto her bus.

"Where have you been you great clutz?" shouted Seth, incensed, as I dragged myself back to my seat. "Why didn't you answer my texts. What a prat."

"Sorry. I met somebody I knew at school and stayed with them for the demo that's all."

"Yeah, well that's no excuse for being an ignoramus. Wazzack!"

"Alright, alright, I said I was sorry."

"Anyway, man, this is Jaz. We got chatting during the demo. I've been telling him all about you. He's wanting to meet you."

Seth had someone already sitting next to him. Jaz was in the row behind and I sidled into the seat alongside. He was clearly a mature student: stocky and clean shaven. He exuded calm as he shook my hand.

"Hi man, Seth's been saying great things about you." From his accent, clearly second or third generation.

"Me? Eh?"

"Yeah, man, your dedication to the Cause. Great stuff, man. Enjoy the march?"

We exchanged a few pleasantries whilst waiting for the bus to depart, then fell silent. The pavement outside was becoming less crowded as people found their buses. Ours looked to be already full but we must have been in a queue waiting to go because we just sat there for an eternity.

I fiddled with my 'Pulse, then gathered up the courage to send Mimi a message. *'Lovely to see you. Meet up back in the city? Michael x.'* Press send. Gone.

All my hopes digitised in space, speeding through the atmosphere, reflected off goodness knows where, finding their way like a crazed Cupid's arrow to Mimi's 'Pulse.

And her heart?

Still nervously waiting for a reply, I sensed motion. The bus was leaving. We were in a convoy and progress was intermittent. I tried to snooze but sleep eluded me. My 'Pulse was annoyingly silent.

I stared out the window past Jaz, who was fiddling with his own 'Pulse. The capital's buildings looked stately and grand, observing our slow departure without comment, unimpressed.

And why should they be impressed? Every week there is a protest in the capital for some reason or other. Each week a bunch of dissatisfied individuals takes to the streets to shout, chant and sing. Who is right and who is wrong? The buildings don't care, these elderly mansions, they have seen it all come and they have seen it all go and yet they remain, always finding plenty of people who compete to take care of them, restore and improve on their magnificence.

Pah! The world's a con. There are those who have and those who don't, and nothing ever changes that. Those who don't have are dissatisfied and march. Those who have construct systems to suppress those who don't have. How to break the system? Impossible, for its tendrils permeate everything and there are many protecting its multi-layered strands.

My 'Pulse was still silent. Hopelessness descended and clung to me like a clammy layer of cling-film. Breathing became difficult and ragged. My eyes fogged and the sights of the capital became unseen, then morphed into the featureless countryside beside the motorway. My body froze, head locked in position facing the window. Mind benumbed, free of thought: a waking sleep.

Jaz jerked me out of my contemplative detachment with a jab of the elbow. I shuddered back to consciousness with a start. Some hours must have passed: it was dark outside, streetlights and headlamps beckoning the way. It looked like we had reached the city; we were already heading towards the centre.

"Hey, man, look at this."

He leant over and showed me a video playing on his 'Pulse. He had the latest model. With a deft flick of his wrist the screen folded up and out so that I could see the image holo. Demonstrators gesticulating, screaming and throwing missiles at a line of spols on horseback. Cut to: more demonstrators, this time chucking bricks through shopfront windows, looting the displays. Cut to: stretchers carrying inert bodies, blood pouring from wounds. It looked as if the injured were spols, judging from the snatches of uniform.

Jaz snatched away his wrist and the screen folded back in. He peered at it himself for a moment, then flicked left.

"Let me read you the news headline, man. 'About 500 demonstrators marched through the capital this afternoon in support of the Cause. The unruly crowd resorted to attacking lines of passive spol officers and general looting. Ten officers have been injured, two seriously. Several protestors and ringleaders have been arrested. The spol has restored calm in the capital.'"

"Eh? Is that meant to be us?" I said, perplexed. "Can't be. There must have been tens of thousands of us there, if not more, and there was no violence."

"Well, you can't be sure of that particular fact, man," said Jaz. "But it was certainly a huge demo, nearer 100,000 if not more from what people were estimating. Some of them are quite experienced; they wouldn't be that far off. It was such a big protest that you'd never see all of it. There could have been trouble behind your portion of the demo. But I doubt there was any violence or looting. I'm sure we won't find anyone who saw any trouble. No, this is pure Government misinformation, belittling and besmirching the Cause. The bastards do it all the time."

"Shit. How can they do that?"

"Easy: they control all the media. They're all in each other's pockets. It's a big mafia. You'll get some of the truth come out over people's individual input on the net before the bastards take it down. But even before then, all it does is recirculate amongst supporters of the Cause: it never gets out to the populace."

"Waste of time protesting then."

"No, it's never a waste of time, because it puts pressure on the buggers, but that's all it does. It loads the system: keeps them on their toes, uses up time and resource. It creates a space for some more effective action to go unseen."

"How do you mean?"

"Direct action, man, direct action."

"Eh?"

"Look, man, we can't talk too much about it here, too many ears, innit? Perhaps we'll meet up back in the city. I'll get Seth to arrange something."

"Just give me your number, Jaz, I'll text you."

"Best not, eh?" he said and touched a finger to his lips in a silence gesture. "Looks as if we're back."

He was right: I could see the college buildings alongside. The bus had slowed. Other buses were ahead, some already parked up.

I checked my 'Pulse – still nothing from Mimi. My spirit popped like a balloon, hope gushing out. The morning had seemed so bright, so full of anticipation and hope. Mimi had been so warm towards me that I had dared to believe we could finally become an item. Then had come my inability to seize the moment. Now, there on the bus, with the morose Jaz depressing me and no sign of a reply from Mimi, there seemed no way forward for us.

Worse was to follow. As we drew up alongside the kerb, I saw her on the pavement, walking away from the Union building. She was alongside a tall, attractive bloke, talking animatedly.

My world imploded.

21 THE BITCH

Despite my affinity for them, the woods and the country park were not the setting for the adventure that changed my life. No, that actually happened right at the heart of the city, in the parkland behind the castle.

The day of the adventure began routinely enough. We had slept in the city centre, breakfasted on leftover pizza, and had wandered into the park in search of lunch. There were many picnickers along the banks of the stream that fed into the city's river. We feasted on titbits and Jake found plenty of abandoned leftovers for his own banquet.

Replete, we moved into the quieter parkland area and settled atop of our favourite mound - the one we'd witnessed the blowtorch attack on the woman from - to observe the world. Jake sat cross-legged, very still, deep in contemplation, eyes open, but observing what? Mullet concentrated on our surroundings for a while, then nestled down, head between paws, and closed her eyes. Only I remained alert, gently sniffing the air one way, then the other, feeling the movement of the breeze, watching the flow of the clouds. Then I too drifted, seeing myself at the bottom of river earth; the atmosphere that enfolded me moving as the water, all eddies and swirls, winds and waves; the universe beyond as the atmosphere. I travelled beyond that river, letting myself flow, breathing in atoms, fruit of the wombs of stars, letting my mind surf waves and currents of energy.

While in this state, I became aware of a presence in the distance, beyond the scent horizon. At first it was manifested as flashes of energy infiltrating the calm of my thoughts. Soon after I picked up a subtle scent that resonated within me. I was instinctively excited by this smell and focussed on it exclusively, pinpointing its exact location.

There.

Mullet and Jake hadn't shifted from their repose. I couldn't wait for them. In fact, something in me wanted to investigate this alone and so I sprinted off towards the luscious aroma, sensing - but ignoring - their questioning gaze darting on my back like laser light as I disappeared into the distance.

I lost the scent's energy signature as soon as I had broken my mental concentration but I was determined to find its origin and continued to beam straight, hoping that whatever had been causing it was not moving much. After three minutes of running across the parkland, as I neared the start of the city's sprawl in the north, I finally reconnected with the aroma. And then I saw the source. It was a bitch. She was alone and trotting towards me. My anticipation grew as we neared. She'd spotted me and had upped her pace. I could feel her excitement and it fuelled mine.

As soon as we met, she was leaping playfully at me, pawing me, nibbling my ears, then moving away, teasing, twisting and thrusting her rump towards me. She was attractive: smooth blonde fur, prissy ears and shapely lines, but it was her scent that intoxicated and consumed all my senses.

I had never been so excited. My tiddly had swollen and was sticking up against my tummy. I could feel it throbbing and pulsating. It felt as though all of my energy was trying to break free through my engorged tiddly, each heartbeat sending a spasmic wave of pleasure through my body. It was affecting my mind too. Reasoning fell away. As the bitch continued to leap and pounce, nibbling at my neck, I became obsessed with the thought of mounting her and rubbing my tiddly against her rear, knowing instinctively that it would heighten the sense of elation that I was experiencing.

I began leaping and twisting with the bitch, timing my jumps when she had her rear to me. In this way I managed to climb onto her rump, my front paws scrabbling to maintain grip on her smooth-haired back. I continued hopping with my back paws, not just to keep pace with her but also to swing my tiddly so that it bounced and grated against her tummy and rump, sending pangs of ecstasy shooting through my body. The sensation surged as my little hops and the bitches' found the same rhythm. My tiddly was no longer bouncing against the bitch but seemed to have disappeared inside her. We continued jauntily bumping against each other for a short while before I began to slobber with the effort, but the sensation was too pleasurable to stop. She started to yelp quietly, I think with pleasure. Then, suddenly, a jolt of lightning shot through my tiddly and reached right up into my body. I thrust myself at the bitch more vigorously, each push rewarded with another surge of glorious feeling.

The pounding became my world. There was nothing other than that feeling pulsing from the bitch, through my tiddly and into my body. I sensed this bliss was generated by the pounding so I thrust even harder and faster. Then I felt an even more intense sensation, like my brain had exploded. My vision turned incandescent white, effectively blinding me temporarily. I stopped breathing and was immobilised, muscle spasms the only motion, and was only vaguely aware of the bitch's yelps quickening. She then leapt forward and twisted, dragging me with her but, through her movement, threw me off her rump so that I ended up with all four paws back on the ground and facing away from her.

Woa, that was weird!

The overwhelming sensation coursing through my body had stopped and I realised that I was once again able to think coherently. I tried to move away from the bitch but was stuck. I strained my body round to see what was happening. My tiddly was still retained within the bitch's rear and I couldn't pull away, no matter how much I tried. She twisted and turned, still excited, and I had no option but to follow suit. After a few minutes of feeling a dope, being pulled this way and that at her whim, she yanked sharply to one side, jumped over my body and stood sassily, staring me in the eye.

I was free. I looked round and down at my tiddly. It was still much larger than normal, swollen and vibrant red, and oozing liquid. I wanted to lick myself clean but was bumped by the bitch, who began her enticing dance of leaps and twists afresh, flaunting her rear, pushing it up into my muzzle, overpowering me with exotic, exciting scent.

I felt tired and would gladly have laid down for a rest but her display aroused me once more. My tiddly surged up and all rational thought ceased. I leapt on the bitch and this time coupling was instant. Intense bursts of pleasure jolted through my body as I pounded enthusiastically, her whining and panting enhancing the thrill. She was strong and held her position despite my forceful thrusting. I soon tired, needing to focus on little leaps from my back paws to get the push for sensation that was driving me on. My panting was becoming more ragged as my mouth opened wide, gulping for air. The same explosion of sensation that I was yearning for didn't seem to be happening this time. Even so, as I pounded and pounded, the bitch became more and more excited, her yelping escalating as my own anxiety increased.

I wanted to dismount and take a moment to rest but I seemed to be held firmly in place. My tiddly was trapped by the bitch again. Eventually, in trying to squirm apart, I managed to leap off her and we ended up side by side. I still couldn't move away and as the bitch continued to twist and squirm we once more ended up rump to rump. No matter how much I jinxed and weaved I couldn't get away, so there we stayed for a few minutes, twerking a circle back to back.

It was only now, as I slowly regained my breath, that I became aware of my surroundings. In my excitement I had blindly run further from the mound than I'd thought. I was nearly at the extreme edge of the park, a place that I'd only been to a couple of times before with Mullet and Jake. It wasn't a popular area with visitors; there were no through paths leading anywhere and the vegetation had been left to grow wild. The setting was more like the woods that were our more frequent haunt than the manicured city centre park. The bitch and I had met in a small natural clearing. Trees and thick bushes - which I had no recollection of passing through in my rush towards her - surrounded us on all sides, making it difficult to see beyond a couple of yards.

We continued our circling, the bitch still retaining my tiddly. My apprehension increased as the afternoon passed away into evening, any pleasure from the encounter long forgotten.

Where are Mullet and Jake? Are they still on the mound? Why have they not come to get me? Surely they would have wanted to move on by now?

Suddenly the bitch became excited again; her rear wiggling excitedly. I sensed why: another dog was approaching. Could it be Mullet? No, that was just wishful thinking. It didn't smell like Mullet and I couldn't sense her, much as I desperately craved for her to be there.

The dog walked through the bushes into the clearing directly in front of me. It was another male. He stood tall, at least a handspan more than me. He had long brown hair flecked with black streaks and a pointy nose and ears. The hair was sleek and meticulously brushed; clearly one of the upper class dogs that we often saw walking on leather leads in the park. I sensed he was both excited to see the bitch and angry at seeing me. He tried circling us to get to the bitch. I resisted, trying to twist so I could keep facing him but, at the same time, the bitch was twisting against me, keen to meet the new dog. The constant tension between us was making my tiddly ache. Reluctantly, I conceded to her, allowing the rotation unopposed, so that she was facing the new arrival.

I could sense through her rhythmic movement and the sound of their panting that they were beginning to play the same games that had so excited me. I tried to break free of her again by doing little leaps with a twist but ended up hurting myself. I couldn't turn around. Straining round to see, I noticed the dog's tiddly had grown and that their games were becoming more tactile. They necked and nibbled at each other's ears, each of them beginning to slobber. When the dog saw me straining to look, he pulled back the skin from his jowl to bare his teeth and jaws, then growled and lunged at my face. I drew back just in time, feeling piercing pain gore my insides from groin to crown as the bitch's grip held firm.

In avoiding the dog's lunge I lost sight of him and the sudden panic lowered my other senses. I felt a painful impact on my rump that knocked me sideways and momentarily off my feet. It was only through my attachment to the bitch that I remained standing, although the pain in my tiddly became excruciating. Agony exploded with vivid colours inflaming my mind, reawakening the memory and the fear that I'd felt in the wheelie bin as a pup.

Have I been transported back in time?

Darkness and terror enfolded my vision in the dappled light of the clearing.

Time flipped, slowed, melded.

Remnants within my brain grappled to stay with the present and tried to follow the dog's movement as vision faded. He bounded round to face me once more and lunged directly at my head, fading and dipping in the last moment before impact. There was no need for such artifice. I felt a piercing pang from my neck as the dog took hold and pulled, then searing burning like a branding iron traversing my insides as the bitch hopped, weaved and twisted in her continuing attempts to entice the dog.

I was a raggedy in a surreal tug-of-war, a victim of the lust enfolding these two.

This cannot be!

I could smell my own blood - or was it the trash from the wheelie bin? My mind spun as I clawed at the darkness, trying to clamber up out of the dank pit. I yelped. No sound came. I kept bumping my nose against an unyielding object. My neck hurt where the dog had clamped its jaws. I felt the vomit in my mouth as I wretched from the rotting pong. Each movement from the bitch was like shrapnel ripping my guts. I yelped, I screamed. I resisted with pure resolve because I had nothing physical left to give.

This cannot be!

I will be free!

And then, in a flash, life afresh, startling in its clarity. My head recoiled backwards as the dog released my neck and simultaneously the shooting pain burning my insides vanished. I was able to breathe normally once more. Vision returned. I stepped back and looked up to see the dog and the bitch both facing me, heads down low, hacks up, growling. But they weren't staring at me: their gaze was fixed on something else beyond me.

It was only then that I sensed her.

Mullet.

Mullet had come to save me once again. Emboldened, and knowing that Mullet would back me up, I took a step towards the now defensive couple. It was enough. Synchronous with my footstep forward they turned and fled, running abreast at speed, disappearing through the dense undergrowth into the wood beyond.

Instinctively, I followed, yelping. I wanted to chase them off into the distance, then return so that Mullet and I could lick my wounds clean without being molested. They were faster than me in my injured condition and were quickly out of sight.

At that moment odd things started to happen. The dogs' scent faded more rapidly than I expected. I was becoming uncertain in which direction to continue the chase when I broke through the vegetation into another clearing. Startled by what I saw, I dug my front paws into the ground and skid to a halt.

It was now clear that I had reached the end of the park. Here, the trees and dense vegetation gave way to a shady, fetid pool, green with algae. This was a quiet spot because the pool made a natural dead-end; there was no way through into the city as the far end was walled off. Dampness and distance made it an unpopular place for visitors and on the few occasions that Mullet, Jake and I had come here, it had always been deserted. However, this time, two men were standing by the shore. Their auras were bright and vivid, enveloping the scene in a mist of pulsating colour.

One man, the shorter one, exuded a swirling red aura as he gesticulated in conversation. This dense mist abutted his friend and frightened me, recalling uncomfortable memories of the attack in the park. The taller man's aura was thinner and more confused, throwing wisps of different colour in short bursts, with a preponderance to yellow. He had heard the rustling sound accompanying my abrupt arrival and turned to look at me, despite the shorter man continuing to talk to him excitedly.

Once again that extraordinary afternoon, time slowed.

And then stopped.

The earth had ceased turning. I sat and unhurriedly studied the man: aura, vibe, scent, feeling, facial features. The scrutiny caused my senses to explode and reverberate within me, churning my stomach and mind.

What's happening to me?

I couldn't converge my jumbled thoughts. I was trembling violently. I felt an immense compulsion to walk up to this man, sit by his side and follow him wherever he might go.

Who is he? And what about Mullet and Jake?

I glanced behind me. Mullet had already entered the clearing and had sat on a mossy mound merely a couple of yards behind me. She was statuesque and made no attempt to beckon me.

Time: anchored, immovable.

I turned my attention back to the taller man once more, who still held me fixed in his gaze. We looked at each other for several lifetimes, not breathing, not blinking.

And then time played on.

The man crouched down slowly, his aura steadying and softening to cool pink, and beckoned me with his outstretched hand, rubbing the tips of his fingers gently together to tempt me over. I looked behind me again, hoping for guidance. Mullet was inscrutable, her aura frozen and unreadable.

What was it that caused my body to move forward? I do not know, but move forward it did, surely without instruction from me, stepping lightly but confidently towards the man, giving a welcome tailwag. I circled him, then turned a couple of nervous circles myself before shuffling my rump down to sit softly by his side.

"There's a good little fella," he whispered, touching me lovingly on the nose.

I had sat facing Mullet and looked at her again.

Mullet?

She saw the man's kindness, stood, turned and walked unhesitatingly away from us back through the dense foliage into the park.

She had not beckoned me to follow.

An empty wind coursed my body, icy barbs causing me to shiver violently, but then the man smoothed my ear, cupped the top of my head with the palm of his hand and ran his finger slowly down between my eyes, down my muzzle and let it rest gently on my nose once more.

"There's a good little fella."

At that precise moment, the world was perfect.

"Come on, Mike, leave the dog alone," said the shorter man.

"Back off, Jaz. Can't you see he's injured? He needs help."

22 ENCOUNTERS

The bile leadening the pit of my stomach wouldn't dissipate. I was in a permanent state of high stress, constantly checking my 'Pulse for a message from Mimi. Couldn't eat, sleep. Nothing. She was the one who had offered to exchange numbers after the demo. I couldn't understand how she could just ignore my message. And who was that tall bloke she had been walking with? Was she going with him? Surely not, or he would have been with her on the demo. Questions, questions, doubts pinballing around my head, shattering peaceful thought.

After a couple of days I texted her again, in the vain hope that my previous message had been swallowed up by the system and never delivered: *'Hi Mimi. Hope u enjoyed the demo. Meet up again sometime :)'*

Still nothing.

The days passed and my 'Pulse remained silent. I struggled with the concept that I might never be one with Mimi or even see her again. Like me, she shunned any social media and I didn't know exactly where she lived, only the vague area. I knew what course she was on, so I could easily stalk her out, then pretend to bump into her accidentally. Yes, that was a plan, though not a palatable one: what if I saw her with the tall Adonis again?

Seth kept shattering any possibility of calm thought during this period. He must have been buoyed up by the demonstration or, more specifically, by Jaz. He kept pestering me about upping my involvement in support of the Cause, nagging, nagging. "Join in direct action," he'd nag all the while. That's what he'd be doing.

"There's no change without a fight," he'd say.

Enervated at the interruptions to my mental machinations over Mimi, I lashed out against the wall, cracking the plaster, hurting my wrist and smashing my 'Pulse.

"Look what you've done, man. Idiot!" shouted Seth.

"Shit!"

How was I to access my messages now? I'd have to get another 'Pulse and that would take days even if I could afford one. Shit.

Seth would not desist, and kept on extolling the value of direct action. I wasn't happy with the concept initially but he began to get through to me. I called it terrorism and he just laughed, starting on a lengthy dissertation of historical figures who'd been branded as such but ended up accepted by 'civilized' society. I batted some of them straight back. The IRA for instance. Alright, so McGuiness had tea with the Queen and Adams shook Charlie's hand, but what the fuck had they achieved? Their island was still divided. The one that he really caught me on though was Mandela. Don't know why, but Mandela had been a big hero of mine since I'd been captivated by that old movie. I had watched it a few times. The scene of his release from prison was one of the biggest emotional highs I had ever experienced and I'd followed up by reading his autobiography. I was struggling to answer Seth. He spotted he'd got me, so shut up and left me to ponder on my own. Mandela burrowed into my brain, sharing it with another impenetrable problem, Mimi.

What difference? What difference had Mandela – the man himself – made? More specifically, what difference had his involvement in direct action made? He was the brains, not the brawn. Not the one who planted the bombs. That didn't make him any less responsible of course, the blood was on his hands. Was Seth right? Can any change ever be enacted without bloodshed, without a war, conventional or otherwise? Would we ever have known about Mandela if he had not been so involved in direct action?

Not a chance!

As a result of his imprisonment, Mandela became the effective icon for his cause.

And what of this modern obsession for suicide bombing as a tactic of war? Was that just a fad or was it driven by circumstance – the theatre of operations - and the weapons available? Indeed, was it a form of conducting a campaign of war for a cause or was it simply an extreme form of protest? It didn't leave the perpetrator in a very strong position. There was cannon fodder and there was cannon fodder - surely?

Was there not a way of enacting change other than through violence? My mother's Catholicism, though it had never been foisted on me, had perhaps had an influence, as had my schooling. Or was it simply down to my nature? It could not be right to kill, especially innocent people just going about their daily lives. Killing was wrong, it caused suffering. Suffering was wrong, it must be avoided.

I couldn't even win the argument with Ghandi.

"What about Ghandi then?"

Ha! Now I've got him.

And I continued triumphantly: "He advocated non-violence. His peaceful resistance defeated the Empire. You do not have to be violent to take direct action: there are other means."

Seth laughed loudly.

"Fool! You know nothing. That was simply the best tactic for that particular situation at that time. The Empire was already crumbling: there was no need for more.

"Ghandi advocated violence if the alternative was cowardice. He expected the nonviolent activist to stand and die for his cause but, if that was not assisting the cause, then the activist should fight. It was a simply tactic of war, like any other. Cowardice was not an option."

There was plenty of evidence from the net to support that general view, even if Seth wasn't being entirely accurate.

So: if we do nothing - more suffering.

As the days passed these thoughts infiltrated my mind more and more, to the extent that they troubled me as much, if not more, than Mimi and her imponderables. Rather than just responding, I started proactively initiating debates with Seth, who always had an answer to everything. Sometimes I could see the flaws in his arguments but other times - equally or more often – not. Then, lying in my bed waiting for illusive sleep, I'd realise that some of my own objections, proffered confidently at the time, were totally inadequate.

Seth was a hardliner. He considered that there were no innocents. Everyone has a choice. If you choose not to become involved, when clearly there are crass injustices on your doorstep, then your choice still condemns you. You cannot opt out. Doing nothing is a choice. Not choosing between the sides is a choice – the wrong choice. He was adamant on this point.

"There's evil out there man, there's evil for everyone to plainly see and if you do nothing about it then you're part of it. You deserve to be eradicated!" he would shout, more than once.

No space to live a peaceful life. Not for Seth. For Seth, everyone was involved: if not for you then against you. Thankfully he drew the line at small children; I'd have had to abandon him there.

I could see that his argument was powerful and difficult to refute. Wasn't what he was saying consistent with Christian teaching? His rants reminded me of the story of the Good Samaritan, a staple of my childhood. It was unequivocal. The priest and the Levite were condemned. They saw the injustice and chose not to act.

Condemned!

Doing nothing is not acceptable.

The problem of arguing with Seth was that he was clearly biased. His mind was fixed. I was struggling with my own convictions, my own thoughts, my own feelings of self worth and I needed someone with a more flexible mind to bounce things off. My musings on the Christian teaching led me to think of the priest at the local church, St. Peter's. I'd heard that he supported the Cause and so I toyed with the idea of having a chat with him. It wouldn't be an easy conversation to broach but a priest would surely be sympathetic and discreet.

This plan made me feel somewhat hypocritical because, as adolescence had turned into early adulthood, I had completely rejected the idea of the Christian God. This omnipotent who demanded to be worshipped every week, under threat of eternal damnation, but who ignored all the callous atrocities in the world he had created. Eh? Worship him? Follow him? Nah. Not for me. I would take my chances.

The problem was, like much else in my mind, I couldn't make my thoughts converge on a satisfactory conclusion. Had the universe just come into being by itself, as the Hawkingites would have us believe? I couldn't quite make that thought focus either. Created, then? By whom or what? God, for the sake of a name: might have been a committee of experts for all I knew. So who had created God? In attempting to rationalise this famous conundrum I fantasised that God himself had been created by some advanced civilization, then travelled back in time to its proto-inception and created the universe.

You think that's crazy? Ha! Go listen to all the religious ideas, I can't see how it's any more whacky than most of them. At least it makes for a logical sequence of events, instead of something popping out of nothing.

Anyway, the point is that, like a lot of other things, I was looking for a spiritual answer to suit me. Catholicism or another Christian faith was not it. Neither was it Lajat, mind. My interest in the Cause was purely humanitarian.

Hypocritical or not, the idea of speaking to the priest flourished in my mind. He had invited a Kudnok to the Easter Sunday service and there had been a march through the street from the Church to the Kroda. Everyone was talking about it. Seth and all our friends thought he was a hero. I'd heard reaction in the street was very positive, although some thuggish graffiti had been daubed on the wall of the presbytery. That was gone now, painted over.

One man's hero, another's villain.

So, I decided to go to mass in the hope that I would get a chance to speak with him afterwards.

Self-conscious paranoia gripped me as I walked down the street to the church. It felt as though I was being watched, as if my plan was clearly visible to all. Lasers burnt in my back: I was a target. I walked on, heart pumping fast, and arrived a few minutes before the service was due to begin. People milled about outside, chatting. Families, mostly, and old women. It seemed as if they all knew each other. It was all very convivial but no-one met my gaze or welcomed me. I had slowed near the entrance, dithering, scanning the scene for a sign of the priest. Not spotting him, I carried on in, taking a seat near the back, on the end of one of the pews.

There was a good attendance. The church must have been about two-thirds full, more than I remembered from my stalking missions years before. I hadn't noticed it then – too focussed on Mimi, I suppose – but the priest had a presence and charisma that was palpable from the moment he entered the church. When he spoke, his words washed through your body, cleansing. If this man believed in God, maybe there really was something in it. The prayers became beautiful and real. I relaxed, joined in the responses and the gestures. The sermon was short. I can't remember what it was about, probably the day's gospel reading; it certainly wasn't about the situation in the city as I had hoped.

When the time for communion came, I again felt self-conscious, and decided to stay in my place, as I did not go to confession and was too embarrassed to ask for a blessing.

Sitting there for those few minutes, more alone than alone, I tried to pray. Concentrating on clearing my mind, I tried to ask God what I should do. And, in the silence of that part of the service, I felt sure that, should I help the Cause, God would help my relationship with Mimi flourish. It was an odd sensation, not an epiphany or anything like that, more of a clearness of mind, a certain conviction, a lifting of confidence.

I still wanted to speak to the priest at the end though. Helping the Cause was the conviction that I felt, but how best to do it? Seth was pushing me towards direct action; I wanted to hear the views of this man. I remembered that it was the custom for the priest to wait outside the church after the mass and talk to members of the congregation, a bit like a tea party, so at the end I filed outside and waited for an opportunity. Again, no-one spoke to me, despite the fact that I was clearly on my own and looking lonely.

I lingered, waiting for an opportunity. Eventually he was free and I moved in quickly before anyone else could accost him. He smiled as I approached. At last: someone had responded to my presence.

"Hello, Father."

"Hello, my son. I've not seen you here before. Welcome."

"Thank you, Father. I was wondering if I would be able to have a chat with you about something?"

"Surely, my son. What's it about? Is it something that we can talk about here or should we go inside?"

Before I could answer, a small child ran past us at speed, stubbed his toe and fell sprawling, screaming as he hit the ground. Everyone stopped talking, but the priest was the first to react, quickly moving to pick the boy up in his arms and soothe him.

"There, there. It's alright little fella, let's see what you've hurt, shall we?"

Then the women moved in. One of them – the mother presumably - positively snatched the child from the priest's arms. A gaggle ensued and I was swept from the scene by the tidal wave of women eager to calm the toddler, who was sobbing again. The priest had now been mobbed and was being jostled. I felt totally marginalised and my self-consciousness returned. It didn't look like I was going to get another opportunity to speak to him anytime soon and so I left, mentally dismissing my scheme as a bad idea.

Walking back, steps as ponderous as my brain's crunching of imponderables, I again felt a strong, unnerving sensation of being watched. I was relieved to arrive back home.

Without the benefit of the priest's advice, it seemed as if my mind had coalesced on the idea of direct action, without being too certain exactly how that should be enacted. Through the strange experience I'd had in the mass, I was now feeling that if I should proceed on that course then my relationship with Mimi would be blessed.

Seth was not slow to pick up on my change of mood and continued to chip away at my remaining doubts. One day – and I'm sure he had organised this in advance, although he never admitted it - when we were walking home from university, taking a long detour through the central park, we happened to come across Jaz, sauntering innocently along on his own. They both expressed surprise at seeing each other but my suspicion that the whole thing had been pre-planned was given further conviction when, after the exchange of a few pleasantries, Seth made some stupid excuse and scarpered off:

"You two carry on walking and chatting, I'm sure you'll have plenty to say to each other."

I was too slow to react and was stuck with Jaz, who grabbed me, gently but firmly, by the elbow and led me off in the opposite direction from Seth, towards the extreme end of the park. It was the first time that I'd seen him since the demonstration in the capital. He waffled on at first but once we'd arrived at a secluded spot he wasted no time in reengaging with the topic that he'd briefly mentioned during the journey home.

"So, have you thought any more about upping your contribution to the Cause by taking some direct action?"

Ah, so that's the ploy.

No dithering: straight to the crux.

“A bit. Seth keeps pestering me about it. But I’m not sure what direct action means to be honest. I wouldn’t know how to go about it.”

“I can help you there. I happen to be in a group organising attacks on various targets nationwide.”

Seth had never intimated anything of the sort. Was he also involved?

He must be.

“Woa! What group is that, then?”

“I can’t tell you that. I will never be able to tell you that. The less you know the safer you, I and many other people will be.”

“Spooks, eh? But what kind of attacks are you talking about, can you tell me that? Terrorist attacks?”

“Not terrorist attacks at all. We target those who harm the Cause. The only thing we want is to be able to live in peace. We target those who would persecute us, frighten our families, drive us out from our homes. They are attacks in our defence and in the defence of the Cause. It’s the only way we can show how determined we are to protect our way of life. I don’t call that terrorist attacks. We are not violent people. We are fighting for our freedom. Freedom – yes – that greatest of values of your society. Can anyone deny us that? We are freedom fighters.”

“But you kill people, yes? Which attacks has your group been responsible for?”

“I can’t tell you which attacks but, yes, we kill people. That’s the only way of convincing people of our determination.”

“Why can’t you simply talk to them? Go through the protest groups, put pressure on the politicians, on the Government. The Cause is a peaceful movement, isn’t it?”

"The only thing that puts pressure on the Government is the fear that they will fall. We're not big enough to do that politically, so we have to show our strength in other ways. Militarily. It is the only way that we will have a voice. The only way that we will be heard."

"But you're not an army."

"Same as, fit for the modern world. Each age has a special way of fighting. This age is no different. We fight with what we have, which is ourselves."

"What do you mean? You use suicide bombers then?"

"We don't use that term. It is demeaning, as though our soldiers don't have the courage or wit to wage what the disparagers would have you believe is the only way to conduct an honourable war. What could be braver or more honourable than laying down one's life for a cause one believes is just? That is what soldiers have done throughout the ages. Sometimes the odds have been stacked against them surviving. Were the soldiers going over the top from the trenches in the First War suicide attackers? No-one calls them that but sometimes they were very nearly that. Much more significant is the fact that they were fighting for a cause they thought to be just. They fought with honour. We too fight with honour in pursuit of our freedom."

"But both sides of that conflict can't have been right. One of the causes must have been wrong."

"Indeed. Perhaps they were both wrong. Anyway, who decides what is right and what is wrong? It's purely down to perspective. That's the dilemma of the world, the dilemma of life. That's why you must search your heart and not be coerced into following a cause, like many conscript soldiers. I'm only talking to you here because you've come to the road of the Cause by your own means. We know this. I believe the Cause is just, and I believe you do also. What we are now doing is giving you an opportunity to act on that belief more directly."

"But I've no wish to die."

"No, none of us have. But, Michael, only one thing is certain from life, and that is death. I'm giving you a choice here – an opportunity even - about how you actually die. Do you wish to grow old, decrepit, drowning without dignity in a pool of shit in your own bed, with only a vague memory of how you could have done something useful with your life? No? Do you want to age gracelessly, too frightened to look in the mirror for fear of seeing your own despotic father mockingly staring back at you? Or are you going to do something worthwhile in pursuit of a just cause that you believe in?"

I hesitated, not for the first time, and Jaz continued unabated:

"Or is it that you're a coward, can't face death, even when you know you'll be helping the Cause?"

A coward?

That word again, causing confusion. Further hesitation, only this time Jaz didn't come to my rescue with another stream of words. I had to form a reply. A coward? Fleeting, painful scenes from the school playground swept through my mind. I felt the blows pummelling Seth's face.

"I don't know to be honest. It's a daunting prospect. I guess that in other forms of action there is at least a chance that you'll survive. What you're suggesting seems so final. And there'd be no way of knowing what the results of your sacrifice will be, whether it will have been worthwhile. I don't have the religious convictions of dahigists. There's no conviction in my mind that my actions will lead me to a better place. It could be the end. It's such drastic action to take without knowing."

"You don't need the religious convictions of a dahigist. This has gone beyond dahig. It's not only the blueheads. We are fighting inhumanity. Inhumanity on a local and on a global scale, performed by Corporations, Governments and the like."

"But I'm too small, too insignificant, I can't take on those massive organisations."

"No, but together we can tackle the local ones and hope to influence the larger ones. What's the saying? 'Look after the pennies and the pounds will look after themselves'. It's the same principle. You've seen how people are treated in the city, the discrimination they experience and the attacks they suffer. You have seen the fear on the faces of the women and children, who simply wish to live in peace. And you do know what effect your action would have. You can work it out, man. All you have to do is to look back at how previous attacks have helped the Cause. They show our fortitude, our strength, our commitment. An attack by one such as yourself, a Caucasian, would be highly significant, demonstrating how the injustices are gaining notoriety even amongst the Christian community. That would make your action worthy. Many more would be recruited to the Cause. You'd be a hero. You'd know that in advance. You'd be remembered, by many more than the followers of the Cause."

"I don't want to be a hero."

"Call it what you will. The point is that you'd be doing something worthwhile with your life. You'd be trading it for an effect that would ripple through millions here on earth both in space and time. Come on, man. Think about it. You know I'm right.

"The time in your life to do something meaningful is now, when you are young, before life turns you fat with greed and lust. You'll get lost in that morass of adulthood as the blubber builds around your bones. Middle age: the drive for money, the push for promotion, the desire for sex. You'll drink too much, your dick will go limp and your wife will leave you for a younger man. Your skin will sag. You'll become another rotten vegetable in this fucking compost heap of a shitty planet. You'll be slumped there all alone in front of your wall monitor in your shitty little house and you'll see some violent injustice unfold before your eyes. And then you'll feel guilt pricking sharply at your conscience, reawakening a distant memory, and you'll know – you'll know, Michael! - that you could and should have done more. But you'll have joined the mass ranks of the guilty by default. You sad bugger, Michael…"

I think I was still listening to Jaz's rants, the words somehow registering in my brain, but what captured my utmost attention was a rustle in the undergrowth behind my left shoulder. I turned away from Jaz. A dog had run into the clearing where we were talking. It was some kind of mongrelly thing and stopped as soon as it had sensed us. It sat down about five yards away and stared at me intently, disconcertingly even, although I felt no threat from it. Another, bigger, dog soon followed the first one into the clearing but stopped on the edge, by the border with the trees, not coming any closer. The first dog kept turning round to check on it, as if unsure of itself.

Jaz could tell that my attention had drifted to the dogs and stopped talking. I was thankful for the silence. I could see that the first dog was injured: there appeared to be streaks of blood on its head and flanks. Slowly, I crouched down and gestured to it, hoping that it would approach closer. With only a slight hesitation, the dog walked up to me, tail wagging, and sat down facing the denser vegetation where his friend still waited placidly. The wounds were fresh and I could see blood oozing onto his muzzle and neck.

"There's a good little fella," I said tenderly, touching him softly on the tip of the nose.

The dog relaxed under my touch. Seeing his contentment, his companion turned and disappeared back into the undergrowth. I continued smoothing the dog's ears, running my hand over his head, over his eyes and onto his muzzle, coming quite close to one of the gaping wounds, but avoiding it. He was totally docile and I could tell that he was loving the attention. He was not wearing a collar and was probably a stray that had evaded the council vans.

"There's a good little fella," I told him again.

Amazingly, this wounded dog had brought me a peace and calm the like of which I had never experienced. At that moment, the world felt right. I just wanted to stay there forever, crouching by this magical creature, sharing love and affection. Never move, never shift, time itself to stand still.

Forever.

"Come on, Mike, leave the dog alone," said Jaz, sounding frustrated.

Pouff.

"Back off, Jaz. Can't you see he's injured? He needs help."

"Concentrate, Michael. Man, this is it. The Cause needs you. This is one of those big special moments that go to define your life. Time moves on, man. Grab it."

"Yea, well, those types of moments have never been kind to me."

"Well, then, even more reason to make this one count. I need an answer, man. Will you help us or no?"

The dog felt content under my touch. He had wedged his head between my knees and was revelling in my caress. I desperately wanted Jaz to shut up.

"Alright, then, yes. Yes!"

Was it me that said that? Must have been, there is no-one else here.

"Good man, shake on it. We'll meet again one more time then. Someone will be in touch about the when and where. Could be weeks, could be months, possibly longer."

"Alright. Now I'm taking this dog to the vet."

"Sure thing, man, but don't get too attached."

PART 3
DECISIONS

23 THE CITY

So…

What do you mean, which city is this? Are you really asking that question after everything that you've seen?

What? What do you mean 'is it London, New York, Rio or Rome?' Have you not understood a thing? Eh? What do you mean, how tall are the buildings? What the hell does size matter? Buildings? You guys are so obsessed with size and machismo displays. Since when has size been a factor?

Here: take a look at this. See if you can spot any difference.

♦ ♦ ♦

The city has grown rapidly in recent years. It now reaches the edge of the marshland, close to where the nats live. Further off, the eksterlanders are expanding their own territory ever nearer. He can feel the tension, as though he is being physically squeezed. The pressure is on to take action. His masters want expansion, new trade. The minister wants new converts, new souls. He himself wants wealth, success, fame.

What to do?

The path of least resistance becomes clear. The nats must be pushed back. They are too close now, becoming too bold, robbing and attacking citizens. Fill the nats with fear, make them retreat from near the city's edge to allow for the attainment of more territory and the peaceful development of the city.

More territory equals more immigrants. More immigrants equals more houses. More houses equals more wealth.

The unleashing of greed.

The relentless pursuit of more.

More!

He gathers a force of soldiers and briefs them. Instil terror into their hearts. They have no souls. They are savage like the beasts that roam the plain. Show no mercy. We have God on our side. May He bless our mission to cleanse this land of heathens.

The soldiers ride out, brazen and confident. They enter the village encampment, three abreast. A group of elders approach to greet them. They stand waiting for the soldiers, hand raised in greeting. The soldiers do not slow. As they approach, those in front goad their horses into a trot and draw their swords. Without a word or pause sharp steel whips through the air, glinting in the sun, decapitating the elders with a single strike.

Pandemonium.

Screams.

The nats scatter, men for their weapons, women and children into hiding. To no avail because the soldiers have not come without a plan. The village has been surrounded. A classic pincer. Soldiers attack from all sides, butchering the surprised nats without mercy. This is a lesson not to forget. Not even the children are spared. Babies and toddlers are thrown into the river and the hapless parents cut to pieces as they dive into the water in an attempt to save them. The children drown or are butchered, gored by the soldiers' swords.

The river is streaked red with blood. Coils of intestine flow downstream. Is it the river itself that has been injured? The soldiers barely pause to wonder, too occupied hunting through the tents, chasing down the final victims.

A few escape. Some always do. It's in the nature of things. It is necessary for the tale to be told, for the terror to spread to others.

The soldiers are happy with their work. They attach a few nat heads to their lances and parade triumphantly back to the city.

He is also delighted and embraces the commander-in-chief. This will have taught the nats a lesson they will never forget. The city will now be free to expand.

Glory be to God!

The soldiers, tired from their toils, still have enough energy for a quick game of kickball. They boot some of the severed heads between them as they wait for the well deserved banquet that is being prepared in their honour.

Time passes.

People come and people go.

The city grows and grows and grows and grows. Outwards, upwards; it grows until nobody living in it can remember the tale of the day the soldiers visited the nat village.

Almost nobody.

♦ ♦ ♦

Well, my friend, didn't I tell you?

Now are you beginning to understand?

24 THE STREET

Night.

All is quiet.

The street is deserted and dark, the stars too high and dim to be of any use, the moon too low. St. Peter is tired, his stained glass windows weary from near constant vigilance. He can feel them dimming and blurring as his thoughts slow. He tries to fight off the sleep that is approaching, focussing again on the corner of the street, switching to doorways, craning to peer over into back yards littered with junk.

Fight, fight against loss of consciousness, St. Peter. There's too much to lose. Too much can happen if you're not watching. And there's too much dirt in that past darkness.

But the tiredness is overwhelming. St. Peter's life force ebbs as a swell of fatigue courses through his stones. He succumbs.

Sleep.

And St. Peter dreams of sleep.

♦ ♦ ♦

Night.

All is quiet.

The garden is deserted. He has wandered off to be alone again, leaving us here in the clearing. It's been a tiring day, a stressful day. A very confusing day. The wine at supper hasn't helped, nor the constant interruption of sleep. My head feels dense, as though it's lolloping uncontrollably around on my neck. It's too fuggy for me to stop and focus. I flop down, succumb to the darkness, let sleep take me once again, welcome it even.

♦ ♦ ♦

"Not again! You lazy layabouts. I told you to keep watch!" He whispers roughly, jostling us awake.

I return to consciousness slowly, drugged with broken sleep. I can't see Him in the dark but sense His anger. He's shaking the others awake now, spittering in their ears:

"The time is at hand. Wake up!"

What's He on about now?

There's something else there too, a presence that I can sense, but can't quite discern.

"Wake up! Come on, move," He commands again. I feel Him thump me on the chest.

Loud rustling of leaves from all around us. Bright torches moving forward from behind the boulders and trees, hurting our eyes. Frightened, I struggle to look through the pain. He has His back to me, facing the soldiers.

Invaders!

"It's done," He says, quietly, apologetically, as if to no one.

We rise up but more soldiers arrive from all sides. It's a trap: we are surrounded. Nowhere to run.

The soldiers stand circling us in the clearing, unmoving. The largest of them steps forward, stops directly in front of Him.

"Who are you looking for?" He says.

Before the soldier can answer, Judas steps forward. He has been hiding behind the invaders. Unhesitatingly, He walks up and embraces Him in greeting. "Teacher," he says.

A shiver runs through me. He has warned us about this.

"No. No!" I scream, grabbing my sword, and surge forward. I take them by surprise, barging Judas out of the way, and lunge for the nearest soldier's throat. The Teacher pushes me as I rush past and, unbalanced, I miss the target. The blade scrapes the side of the soldier's head and I fall flat in the dirt from the momentum of the misdirected thrust. The soldiers move towards me, swords at the ready.

"Stop!" He screams. "It's me you want. Leave these others alone."

The soldiers hesitate and the others take their chance, scarpering through the line, then running ignominiously on down the hill. The leader orders the soldiers not to give chase, then kicks me in the ribs, disdainfully. The back of my head thuds against a rock.

"We're done here. Let's go. Back to the house," he orders. "Just bring him. Leave hero boy behind." He spits at me. The gob dribbles into my eye.

They pin His arms behind His back and push Him roughly down the path towards the city. The last of the invaders to leave gives me a strong kick as a farewell. I go sprawling again, getting a mouthful of earth this time.

I splutter and cough, then breathe deep to regain composure. There's no sign of the others. I call. No reply. I can still occasionally see flashes of the invaders' torches and instinctively decide to go after them. Where are they taking Him?

The path is rough and I stumble. Luckily we're soon into the city where the light is better and I can easily track them at a distance.

They take Him into the High Priest's house. The courtyard entrance is unguarded and I sneak in. It looks like they've already taken Him inside, judging by the number of invaders standing guard at the door. I loiter, uncertain what to do. Doesn't look like I can get Him out, not on my own, not without the others. It doesn't look good.

A woman taps me on the shoulder, startling me and I shriek involuntarily.

"Hey! Aren't you one of his followers? You know the man they've just taken into the Priest's house. What are you doing here?"

"What? I don't know Him. Who? What are you talking about?"

I shuffle off back outside, hide in the shadows for a while, trying to resolve what to do. Is there anything I can do? I lean against a wall, breathe deep. My ribs still hurt and I open my mouth to swallow air, in preference to breathing it. Condensation clouds billow up, coloured in the reflected light. The night is cold. It penetrates through to my bones now that I'm standing still and I start to shiver. Uncertain of what to do I gravitate back into the courtyard. I can't see the woman but some other people are standing round a fire, warming themselves. It's too much to resist and I sidle nearer, shielding my face into my hood, trying to look inconspicuous.

The fire is warm and welcoming. I relax in its glow and soon feel rejuvenated. They're talking about the Teacher and speculating about the interrogation they suppose He's being subjected to inside. I join in the chatter, hoping to learn some useful information. Initially it seems as if, unlike the woman, they suspect nothing but then one of them says:

"Wait a moment! I've seen you before – in the riot at the Temple. You were with him when you all went berserk and terrified everyone."

"What?" I shout. "Who? No. No! I've never seen Him, this Teacher you're talking about. Never!"

"Yes you have!" he insists, and I turn away, wanting to flee back towards the street, only to bump into the woman who'd challenged me before. She grabs my sleeve and I resist, stop and look at her.

"Yes, yes, it was you. I'm sure of it. You were with the terrorist!" she says.

The man grabs my other arm:

"Yes, you even speak in that funny accent. You're one of his followers. You're in his terror cell. Ha ha, he's had it now. You've all had it!"

I dig my heel into his foot and, when he jerks, butt him in the face with the back of my head. I twist and yank my arms loose. The woman goes sprawling to the ground but I'm running away, not stopping to see if she's alright. Defiantly now I shout out into the night air: "I don't know Him!"

"I don't know Him, I don't know Him," now as I blubber into my sleeves, back in the darkness of the garden. "He's gone. They've taken Him. I don't know Him."

"I DON'T KNOW HIM!" I scream into the darkness.

Coward, St. Peter.

Coward!

♦ ♦ ♦

"I! DON'T! KNOW! HIMMMM!"

The screams wake St. Peter up from his nightmare.

Not again. Will I ever rid myself of that ghastly dream?

He is perspiring freely from the fear, condensation running down his pillars, dew drops forming on the pews. He shivers, ringing his bells.

The residents of the street are roused from sleep with the pealing and assume that it's the call for early morning mass. Opening their eyes they can see that pre-dawn reflected sunlight has infiltrated the turmoil of night, banishing its terror.

And, with terror departed, coherent thought begins to subdue the dread of the world of dreams. Patterns emerge, ideas, plans, memories.

St. Peter clears his mind. What dastardly deeds could have happened in the street whilst he slept?

Away!

He blows the shame of his slumbers from his steeple, gloomy thoughts dispersing like fog under sunlight. He remembers his mission. He mustn't let Him down now, not again. Repel the invaders. Restore the faith. Become the strong fisherman of men that the Teacher always wanted him to be.

So, what's happening? The street is quiet. Empty. No-one about. All in their beds still. St. Peter breathes a sigh of relief. It looks as if, this time, nothing bad has happened whilst he slept.

He looks inward now, searching for Father Cuthbert. There he is, exactly where St. Peter expected to find him, already up, praying in his room.

Ha! He may well pray, but it won't do him any good, not after the mess he's landed himself in with the Bishop.

St. Peter chuckles, shimmering his bells once more. His plan had come to fruition better than even he had dared to hope. He'd concentrated with all his power to force the child to fall near Father Cuthbert and the women's reaction had exceeded his expectations. The priest had come to the child's aid, of course, picked him up and soothed him, just as St. Peter had expected. The women had swooped on him like piranhas, dragged the unfortunate boy from his arms and virtually accused him of groping. It made St. Peter smile across his broad transept.

Strange days.

To be sure, St. Peter had only anticipated denting the priest's reputation by implicating him in some way with the child's fall, but it looked as if the incident would lead to his total ruination. He knew that the priest had not intended to harm the child, only nurture him, but St. Peter didn't care. Father Cuthbert had had it coming, with his do-gooding and his talk of peace and love. Worst of all was his pandering to those eksterlander tembusi heathens.

One true God. Ours! Enough of this syncretic claptrap, let's say it how it is.

Well, now it looked as if the Bishop would defrock him. The boy's mother and a number of other women had complained. Mrs. Smith had organised them into a formidable protesting unit. St. Peter had overheard them at the Wednesday coffee morning. They wouldn't drop the issue. If the Bishop had a better opinion of Father Cuthbert then he might have supported him. As it was, that treacherous pandering to the Kudnok had sealed his fate. The Bishop was definitely taking no chances of enduring a scandal for this soft-bellied traitor. He had given the women a promise. His machinations to oust the priest were progressing slowly and carefully but soon all the necessary requirements would be in place. St. Peter could wait: he was used to the slow, but irresistible, grind of time. Father Cuthbert was as good as gone.

The quiet of the street is shattered by the joyous pealing of bells. Interminable bells. Disturbed, Father Cuthbert arises from his meditation position and rubs the numbness from his calves.

Blast those campanologists, he thinks, trudging into the kitchen for his morning muesli.

25 THE BOND

Even looking back on it now it is surprising to remember just how strong my bond to Michael was, despite our short temporal association in that life. I play the memories back over again and again, those moments we shared together as clear as limpid sunlight, the sensation of unity as strong now as then.

It's as if we were one from the outset, each of us so much more comfortable in the world when we were together than when apart. That's how it felt, instantaneously, from the moment we met by the pool. I was only ever at peace when enveloped by him; yearning was a constant nagging sensation when he was absent.

That's it. That's the word.

Enveloped.

I could always anticipate his return, sense him from afar and I would ready myself to see and greet him. One day, as I was waiting by the front door, my perception must have been piqued because I could see my own aura extend out beyond the closed door - as though the door didn't exist at all – and out into the tiny yard and then beyond the gate into the street itself. I was marvelling at this sensation when I felt – palpably – the edge of my aura being touched. I knew unequivocally that it was Michael's own aura, reaching out and touching mine as he approached home. The colour of his aura engulfed mine, like a tide covering the land, until it enveloped me completely, so that I was in his presence before he had physically arrived. Our greeting that day was effusive, but then I suppose it always was. He crouched down and I jumped up with joy, wrapping my paws round his shoulders, letting him hug me.

"Willow! Little fella. Great to see you. How ya been?"

My perception was not always so strong, or perhaps it was the aura that was not always so vibrant. To be honest, I'm still not exactly sure how all that stuff works. One is constantly searching and learning. However it happened, that sense of envelopment in his presence, of being part of another conscience, was a constant.

Does that strength of bond go some way towards explaining my desertion of Mullet and Jake? I know what you're thinking, that I'm cheap with my favours, abandoning those who rescued me as a pup and then fostered me into adulthood through the vagaries of the world. They loved and fed me and I abandoned them on a whim for a no-one. Yes, a no-one. Who was he? Some bloke in the park.

How could such a thing have happened? And yet I'm certain that Mullet had given her silent assent to my leaving with Michael. I had felt her acknowledgement as she sat in the clearing. It's another feeling that I remember with absolute certainty.

It won't make you think any better of me but I still feel guilt pangs about leaving Mullet and Jake, all the way through to this present time, despite knowing that they accepted what I did without any rancour. I experience these sensations sometimes when I'm meditating, accompanied by a feeling that my breathing has stopped, and I have to struggle to regain control and clear my mind. Leaving them both is now a part of me. That action follows me – or does it precede me? - down the pathways of time. Like all actions, it's always there, there's no undoing it.

Accept it, learn, move on.

Michael and I were no match for time, succumbing to its uncompromising demands as our life together evolved, the closeness we felt an antidote to less pleasant feelings. That closeness - our bond – was the one thing that time could not touch.

All things considered, that life we shared together was fairly mundane and routine. I guess you might call it 'normal'. It didn't start very auspiciously however. Michael was so concerned about my wounds that he took me to the vet even before introducing me to his own home.

I'd never been to a vet's surgery before. It was very white and very surgical. There was a strong smell of disinfectant that made me feel queasy.

I couldn't help it.

Was it the accumulated excitement and stress of the day? One moment I was standing there, quaking slightly at the strangeness of it all, then suddenly I felt the world spinning round much faster than normal. That's when I vomited all over the sparkling clean floor. Primly dressed nurses began running back and forth with mops and buckets as I wobbled on my feet, trying to regain my composure. It was no use. I felt very tired at that moment and craved sleep, regardless of the mayhem. I flopped onto the floor, legs stretched out front and back, like a prize rug.

"Poor little fella," said Michael, stroking gently at my ears. "It's alright, the vet's going to make you feel better soon. Hold on in there."

He carried on making comforting glurging noises and babbling at me until the vet was ready to see us. More comforting than all the vocalising was his simple presence, like a warm and snug jacket on the coldest of days.

The vet was a lady with a calm and peaceful aura. We started off well: she offered me a very tasty titbit from a plastic bowl that sat on the windowsill of the small consulting room. Then she proceeded to inspect me all over, always touching gently and asking for permission before intruding in more sensitive places. Very polite. She concentrated around my legs, neck and head, where there was a fair amount of blood still oozing from open wounds, matting my fur. One of the nurses came in and together they bathed the wounds. They then bandaged both my front legs. As Michael seemed happy with this procedure and I was still feeling a little woozy I allowed them to continue with it. Actually, I was quite enjoying the attention until they placed this very peculiar plastic cone over my head and tied it to my neck.

Hey!

I did not like that. It was chafing against the wounds if I tried to move and I couldn't see properly to the sides. My world had turned white. Every time I turned to look I bumped my nose into this pesky object. I struggled against it but couldn't shake it off.

"He'll get used to it," said the vet.

"Thanks," said Michael.

Eh? Michael? You're meant to be on my side.

"Pick up the tablets from reception as you're paying."

Needless to say, we were not more than a hundred yards down the road from the vet before I'd managed to wreck the hood. It wasn't difficult. I bashed it and scraped it against every object at every step of the way, heedless of pain, until Michael, exasperated, removed it and chucked it in a bin. He then replaced my new collar, loosening it slightly to lessen the chafing, and reclipped the lead. I'd never walked on a lead before but had seen plenty of other dogs around the city doing it. I was walking to heel straight away: it was easy. There was no need for it though. I would have followed Michael closely, even on that first day. He was very pleased with my compliant behaviour once the plastic contraption had been disposed of:

"What a good boy, Willow. Willow. Willow."

Willow. Clearly he'd decided to rename me from 'little fella,' which is how I'd always been known. He probably didn't realise that I had a name in my life prior to meeting him. Whatever, Willow was fine by me.

Arriving at Michael's home came as a big surprise. Should it have been? I now wonder whether I should have predicted the fact. But who can tell what charades fate will play?

Ha! Nothing, nothing is random.

Not that the house was anything fancy, not at all in fact, more like your normal dingy student accommodation: cluttered, messy, dirty even. The surprise was that he lived in the street where I'd been holed up in the wheelie bin as a pup and where Mullet, Jake and I had occasionally taken refuge at Father Cuthbert's church. Some bad memories, outweighed by pleasant ones.

I didn't much take to his flatmates from the very beginning. Their auras were suspiciously coloured and swirled dangerously. The feeling was clearly mutual. They did their utmost to avoid me and certainly never once looked me directly in the eyes. Their aloofness suited us fine. Michael and I developed our own routines, never having to interact or socialise with them.

My life with Michael was replete with happy memories, full of good times. He would often go out on his own for a few hours in the morning but would invariably return before lunch. I would sleep in until he was about to arrive, then we'd be together for the rest of the day. He thought I was very thin when we met. He'd spoken about it to the vet, who'd agreed, and he put me on three meals a day, served at regular times, something I'd not experienced before but definitely something I can recommend. I had soon put on some pounds and Michael had to increase my exercise. If the weather was dry we'd often play football at the rec. If not, then we'd relax in the bedroom listening to music. Michael had good taste in music.

Priceless moments.

And, of course, it was with Michael that I experienced my first epiphany.

26 THE BOND

I had always wanted a dog. Always. One of my earliest memories – before we had moved to the city - is visiting a cousin's house with my parents for a meal. I hadn't known it before we arrived but my cousin's family had a dog, a young black Labrador called Tattoo.

I was besotted and spent the whole evening focussed on this marvellous beast. It wasn't all plain sailing though. I remember that during dinner Tattoo was served his own meal alongside the dining table, adjacent to where I was sitting. I reached down to stroke his head and he growled menacingly, hackles up, without removing his muzzle from the bowl.

"Miguel! Never touch a dog whilst he is eating," explained my aunt.

Sensible advice, which I was soon to ignore with Willow. You have to learn and grow by making your own mistakes, not simply by listening to what others tell you. I sensed with complete conviction that Willow was totally docile. That proved to be right: he was far more accepting of my intrusions than Tattoo. Never once did he show the slightest aggression towards me.

It's just one of those things isn't it? Where did that hankering for a dog come from? Was it a child's teddy-bear extension? Who knows? Regardless, it was an unrequited hankering that I carried through my childhood: another rucksack of rocks of desire weighing me down on the road of life, hampering my progress.

"It wouldn't be fair," said my parents. "We go on holiday for too long in the summer and the dog would suffer in kennels. Anyway, we can't afford it."

But… I didn't want to go on such long holidays in the summer.

So we had no dog. It was a similar economic justification to the one they presented when I asked if I could have a brother or a sister. Mind you, I'd have preferred the dog over a sibling, no argument.

Alone.

I'd be travelling alone, with just my thoughts for company.

On one occasion when I was in my early teens my parents nearly succumbed to my pleading. It was a sunny Sunday and we'd gone to the park in the centre of the city – the same park that I eventually met Willow in. Half the city must have been there. It was full of families enjoying the warm day. I saw the puppy off in the distance, playing around, running circles around a couple of adults, chasing a ball but not yet clever enough to return it to its owners.

Ignoring my parents' yells, I ran off in its direction. The puppy liked me and we played like young spirits. Running. Tag. Jumping. Cuddling. Licking.

The park folded in on itself, becoming only this small bubble in space where the puppy and I played. Even the sky seemed to lower from the firmament, encapsulating us in the warmth of the sun. The grass was soft to our rolling and tumbling, cushioning our falls. It was a golden moment of my childhood, always fondly remembered.

But time tripped me up – and not for the last time – the lowering sun indicating to my parents that we ought to be returning home.

I pleaded with them that we should keep the puppy. They had become friendly with the other couple whilst we had been playing. The puppy was for sale, the last of a litter. My parents were clearly tempted: I could see that even they had been moved by how I'd responded to the puppy. Tempted they might have been, but ultimately they were resolute.

"It's a bitch," they said. "Too much worry and hassle, or we'd have to spay. Too expensive."

Deflated and alone.

Broken.

I hid in my room.

Seeing Willow that day by the pool broke me again. I lost control of my mind. Whatever resolve I'd had to resist Jaz's persistence evaporated as I communed with Willow. I was transfixed by the powerful emotions that I could sense emanating from him. I had to focus on that, not on Jaz and his schemes. Acquiescence had shut him up.

As soon as Willow had arrived his presence had supercharged all my senses. They resonated with his, causing me to become highly sensitive to my surroundings. The ethereal nature of the pool algae covering its surface, a green blanket undulating softly as insects perforated the surface for air. The sky above this clearing in the park, its colour altered by the funnelling of light within. Willow and I sat at its centre as though lit by a floodlight on a stage. The hum of traffic in the distance like the breathing and shuffling of an audience pent with suspense, ready for the next action to ensue.

Willow had sat down, calm as the pool. And, confident as the experienced actor in the play, he stood and walked over to me unhesitatingly, nestling into me.

Solace descended.

The curtain fell and my life began as if anew.

Willow – I christened him there and then, his name inspired by the trees surrounding the pool – needed to see a vet to clean up and check out his wounds. He looked as though he had been in a fight. It couldn't have been with the other dog that had followed him into the clearing because there had been no blood on that other one and there had been no animosity between the two. I remember seeing that dog once again, in the distance, the day that Willow had an anxiety attack.

He was scrawny, his ribs far too prominent along his flank. No collar. Clearly an undernourished stray who had managed to evade the council vans. I had concocted an emergency leash from my shoelaces and led him off to a vet's practice near the centre that I often passed on the way to uni. Willow did not pull on the lead at all: he walked perfectly to heel, which surprised me.

Luckily the wounds were only superficial. The vet administered a jab of antibiotics, prescribed some tablets and recommended a special diet to build up his body tone.

Unlike me, my flatmates were not at all impressed with Willow. Understatement! They were absolutely livid when I brought him home and started shouting and screaming at me to get rid.

"You're not supposed to have that in here. What if the landlord finds out? Get the mangy thing out."

Willow was already having an effect on me: I was cool and collected in reply.

"Shut it, Seth! You owe me one. He's staying. Finito."

There was more carping from them but it was sporadic and mostly laughable. No sensible landlord would worry about a pet trashing his house when he had rented it out to a bunch of students. Ha! In any case, they could sense how determined I was that Willow was staying. He had instantly become an integral part of my life.

So, reluctantly, they accepted him as part of the household. Luckily Willow was very well behaved, never messed and only ever came out of my room in my absence in order to greet me at the front door.

I did occasionally have to leave him behind to attend some exams and lectures during term but, apart from that, we were always together. I altered my whole routine around him. No job during the summer holiday. No more coffee bars, no more studying in the luxury and calm of the library. No more parties, no more trips to the union bar. It wasn't a problem: I had always felt like a carp on the bank in those sorts of situations. I wouldn't miss them at all. No, I cut my time away from Willow to the bare minimum. I tidied my room to give myself a working space and ourselves some floor space. Willow and I took our meals together in there. He was my constant companion and even slept on my bed. If he ever felt that I was ignoring him and becoming too withdrawn into my own thoughts then he would place his paw on me and break the abstraction. I guess in a way he would be seen as a very demanding dog, although it never felt that way at the time.

Willow always seemed to know what I was thinking or what I was going to do before even I did. I remember that first day after we'd met. I had a lecture to attend so I took him for a walk beforehand, hoping that he'd settle quietly in my absence. Then I shut him in my room and went out. Later, Seth told me that Willow had opened the door within seconds of my leaving and had wandered out into the hall. Seth had heard the noise of the door slamming open and had gone to check on what was happening. Willow was back in my room, lying quietly on the floor, head between paws, looking intently through the open door out into the hall. Seth closed the door to the bedroom and made to leave but within seconds Willow had opened it again. He just sat there, glaring, as if daring him to close it again. As he seemed quiet enough and happy to be in the room itself, Seth decided to leave the door open and monitor the situation.

Willow was still for about ninety minutes, then moved to sit by the front door. Seth says that Willow gave him such a stare that he left him alone. I was home within about ten minutes and he greeted me effusively, spinning and spinning, and jumping up for a hug.

This behaviour became his routine.

“Man, that dog is spooky. S-P-O-O-K-Y,” said Seth with conviction after Willow had been with me a while. “He always knows when you’re coming home.”

Seth was right. Willow was doing it even before he could have learnt my routine. One day I messed around with it on purpose just to see what Willow would do. I’d tipped Seth off so that he could observe Willow carefully. Same thing as always: lie on the floor looking at the door, then move to the front door 10 minutes before I was home.

Cool dog.

We may not have known each other for very long but he was the best friend that I ever had. Without a doubt. He never asked for anything, never nagged. He was always happy to see me after an absence, regardless of its duration; always perfectly content in my company. He accepted me for what I was. If there were any unpleasant aspects to my character then he never showed any diffidence or disdain. His complete confidence in me made me feel, for the first time in my life, content.

Yes, content, as perfect a state as one can hope to achieve in a life. He was the same, to the extent that I envisioned that he was exuding the feeling outwards, blanketing me in its warmth, wrapping me in his unconditional love.

Willow was the perfect antidote for the troubles and concerns in my life. Have you forgotten? I hadn't: the incredible commitment that I had just made to Jaz.

I know that when I made it I was already bewitched by Willow, and the exact details of what was said are muddled by the thoughts and feelings swirling through my brain as a result, but I'm sure that I'd agreed to be a sleeper for his direct action organisation. It was a thought I shied away from because of the turmoil it brought to my mind. Willow helped me to do this. I had to help him recover from his wounds, plan how to build up his body tone, enhance his overall health and keep him amused. He responded in such a positive way that he filled my life with the succour that I'd never had before. He even managed to push Mimi to the recesses of my mind and I stopped looking for ways to re-establish contact after her failure to return my messages from the day of the demo.

There was, as ever in that life of mine, a downside. I was happy, yes, but what would happen if Jaz called in the commitment I had given? I had been left in no doubt that there was no going back, no second chance. I was in, part of their setup, would be bound to their rules. I had no idea of the timescale involved. Was it weeks? Months or years? From what I'd gleamed from various sources, it could be any of those… or perhaps never. Was it cowardly to hope for the latter? More importantly, what would happen to Willow if Jaz called?

That was the question I dreaded appearing in my dreams.

27 A PASSING

We were returning home one day after football at the rec when I felt a foreboding as we approached the street. The sensation came on suddenly, as if some mystical being above had thrown a thick blanket over me. I experienced a weighing down of mind. My brain felt as if it was being squeezed tight, gripped by a vice. The disconcerting foreboding had an additional, and more obvious, physical effect. I had difficulty making headway, as if I was suddenly wading through deep water rather than simply trotting along the pavement.

I hesitated, then stopped, sitting back on my haunches, trying to understand the abnormal nature of what was happening. Michael hadn't noticed anything and continued walking, blanketed only by the weight of his thoughts, so that my lead tensioned suddenly and fell from his loose grip with the jerk.

"Willow? What're you doing?"

I must have looked anxious because Michael sensed my change of mood and immediately became gentler.

"You alright, little fella?" He crouched down and smoothed the fur on my chest. He knew I absolutely adored that. "You look spooked."

The burdensome sensation persisted. I could feel it physically exerting a force against my body, discouraging me from standing up and moving forward. I couldn't smell, hear or see anything that gave me a clue as to what might be happening. I was perplexed.

"Come on, Willow, let's go home. You'll feel better when we're inside."

I didn't budge, even when he tugged sternly on the lead.

"Come on!"

Michael yanked hard on the lead in trying to make me move, which was very unusual, as he was normally quite placid. I tried to comply, concentrating, focussing my thoughts, forcing my legs into motion. We set off again, slowly. His own gait seemed to be normal but I continued to struggle against the treaclish force and was soon panting heavily with the extreme effort needed to keep up.

Head down, all my focus intent on bearing against the pressure, I only belatedly recognised the scent of the street as we turned the corner.

Bang!

It was like walking out of a shelter into a storm. The effect was magnified as we stepped into the street. I stopped and sat back from the shock, causing Michael to drop the lead again.

"Come on, Willow. Move! What's up with you today?"

At least the source of the force had now become obvious. I sat facing St. Peter's church: it was coming from there.

"Willow!"

I wasn't yet ready to move and held firm. Michael was concerned and knelt down, again coming down to my level to comfort me. I could tell that he still couldn't sense anything, couldn't feel that anything was different. Whatever it was, the forceful sensation wasn't a part of his world. I found that odd, but didn't have time to dwell on the reasons why, because time, on this occasion, played on.

There, some thirty yards ahead, atop the steps at the entrance to the church porch, sat Mullet, very still, unnaturally still, immobile even. I had not sensed her before seeing her because of the heavy foreboding. Beyond her, in the dusky, dusty porch from whence the light was banished at this time of evening, I sensed the spirit of Jake, as weak as a famished and thirsty bird grovelling on barren soil.

As I watched, an aural mist emanated from the porch and swept the entrance around Mullet. It enveloped her in a soft embrace, then coalesced into a thin strand alongside her, rising briefly, then swooped down to ground again and darted quickly towards us. I felt its love as the aura slithered between my paws and twirled around my neck, before shooting up, fast as a rocket, high into the sky.

I felt the love and I knew that Jake was passing. Passing into the next realm.

In that instant, the burdensome force vanished and I was up and away, rushing towards the church, dragging the lead behind me. Surprised by my sudden movement, Michael was left rooted to the spot. In his kneeling position, alone there on the pavement, it looked as if he had been teleported from a pew in St. Peter's and unceremoniously dumped on the street.

Mullet didn't move. I slowed as I approached her, licked her ear in greeting and then walked softly past into the porch. Jake half-lay on a travel mat, propped up against the stone wall, in the same posture that I'd first seen him in all those years ago. He was barely breathing. More significantly, for the first time since I'd developed the ability to sense them, he had no aura. I realised that, anticipating the end, his spirit had already departed on its onward journey.

Ears drooped and tail firmly between my legs, I turned, preparing to go back down the steps and rejoin Michael. He had remained near the corner of the street and was yelling and whistling for me to return. Mullet had already gone. She had vanished in the short period that I had been within the porch. I scented up and down the street but couldn't detect her at all: not a trace.

I would never again meet her in that life.

As I started to trot back I heard the door of the church open and hesitated. Keeping quiet, I peered back into the porch. Father Cuthbert was kneeling alongside Jake's body. He made the sign of the cross on Jake's forehead, kissed him gently, closed his eyes and then settled into quiet prayer alongside.

I bowed my head and finally headed on back to Michael, crawling, belly scraping the pavement in apology.

"About time. What's up with you, eh? You alright? Let's go home, see if you're better there."

We walked the short way home in silence. The foreboding had gone and with it any resistance to movement. Despite my sadness, I felt super-light and airy after the burdensome feeling but was keen to get home and collapse into sleep. I bolted one last time, again taking Michael by surprise, and rushed on ahead, into the tiny yard and began pawing frantically at the front door, anxious to get in.

"Jeez!" said Michael, catching up and releasing the lock.

♦ ♦ ♦

I lay on my bed and closed my eyes, trying to recreate the feeling of the loving presence that had enveloped me near the church, but all I could sense was emptiness, hollowness.

I opened my eyes again and scanned the bedroom, now lit only by the faint glow from the reflected city centre lights on the cloud base.

Stillness. Nothing stirred, the silence bouncing off the walls like a tumultuous cry of anguish, terrifying in its intensity.

Jake.

Jake: he who had nurtured and loved me dearly was gone.

Gone.

I howled deep and long, buried myself under my bedding, then lay still, focussing on my heartbeat, waiting for sleep and a new day.

28 SURPRISES

"Mimi!"

No exclamation could ever convey the mixture of surprise and elation that I felt at that glorious, unprecedented moment.

"Mimi."

I was rendered speechless, yet again.

"Hello, Michael. Found you at last. Aren't you going to ask me in?"

"Of course, of course. Come in, come in." But I stood there in the narrow hallway, blocking the way, flummoxed by this situation that I hadn't mentally prepared for.

Mimi salvaged the situation:

"Oh, Michael! I didn't know that you had a dog. How cute."

Willow had naturally followed me into the hallway and sat behind me contentedly, wagging his tail, sporting his 'super-cute' look.

I stood sideways, back firmly against the wall, allowing Mimi to enter, revelling in the sensation as she moved alongside me. I breathed deep, letting her aroma suffuse through each and every one of my cells. I was in heaven.

Mimi knelt down and stroked Willow. "What's he called, Michael? What a cute dog."

She was clearly besotted with him.

"Willow. I found him lost in the park. He was all cut up and bleeding from a fight I think. And scrawny. All his ribs were showing.

I had to take him to the vet to get him looked at. He's looking much better now."

"Oh, he's gorgeous." She fussed him some more, ruffled his ears and gave him a kiss on the nose. "Oh, that's fantastic that you've got a dog. I love animals."

Really? What a stroke of luck.

"Have you got one, Mimi?"

"No, no. The landlord won't have it."

"Well, we've not actually told ours about Willow. He's very well behaved though, doesn't mess the place up."

"Not like your masters, eh, Willow?" she said, continuing to pamper him. Willow was loving the attention. I was beginning to get jealous.

"Would you like a drink? Tea? Coffee? Something stronger?"

"Please. Why not? Just tea will do – no milk."

"No milk? Sure?"

"Sure, I don't drink milk."

"Oh."

I cast a quick glance in the sitting room. Chaos. I couldn't invite Mimi in there. It looked as though Seth and Tom hadn't tidied the place in months. Not making excuses but I didn't go in there anymore; not since Willow had arrived.

We couldn't continue standing in the entrance hall: by default Mimi followed me into the kitchen. Another tip.

She could see the anxiety etched in my face. "Don't worry, Michael. I live in a student house too, don't forget."

"Sorry, it's awful. I rarely stray out of my room because of Willow. No excuse, I know."

"I shall expect to find that in perfect order then," she stated confidently and chuckled lightly. The sound was like that of a warm breeze gently tickling the soft underbelly of fresh spring leaves. I loved that sound, had heard it often in school days. It was a warm, wrap-around sound, an engulfing, comforting sound. It had been absent on the day of the demo. The seriousness of the event, together with my own tension had precluded a soft conviviality between us. This was a different Mimi, relaxed and confident.

"You're a difficult man to track down, Michael. It's taken me six months to find you. Nowhere to be found on the net. And your mother was no help at all. I called by during the summer holidays to ask for your address but she slammed the door shut in my face."

"What? I'm so sorry, Mimi."

Racist bitch.

"But, Mimi, I texted you after the demo, a couple of times. I'm sure it was the right number."

"I lost my 'Pulse, or it was stolen in the crush trying to get back on the bus. When I went to text you from my seat, it was gone. I hadn't even noticed that it was missing in the crush. Must have been someone in the crowd. "

"Have you managed to get it back?"

"No. Gone. I didn't have insurance and the company wouldn't give me a new one. I've only recently managed to buy one. It's not as fancy as the other one but it'll do."

"Oh, you on the same number?"

"No, they wouldn't let me have that either. Something to do with the fraud investigation."

She wasn't ignoring my calls. There's hope.

"Let's take these drinks in my room. It's tidier. And I've got biscuits in there."

Willow led the way, opening the door for us.

"Clever dog. Oh, very good, Michael, very neat and tidy. Impressed."

"Thanks. It's actually easier this way. Willow and I are in here most of the time. Well, when we're not walking on the rec, anyway."

"Do you take him into lectures with you?"

"No." I'd never thought of trying. It was a good idea. "He stays in the room with the door open. He likes to watch the front door 'til I'm back."

"Ah. Clever dog." More ear stroking, then Willow rolled over to have his tummy tickled.

"We could take him for a walk round the rec if you like?" I suggested, heart thumping wildly, surprising myself with my audacity.

"I can't right now Michael. I've got a lecture. I'd love to some other time though. I only popped round to invite you to a dinner party we're having round at ours on Thursday. A week today. Just a few friends, you know."

Wow!

"I'd love to come."

"Of course, Willow is invited. Though I suspect he'll totally steal the show. I will warn you though, Michael, it'll be vegan."

"Vegan?"

"Yes, vegan. You know: one up from veggie. No cheese, no eggs. Nothing that is a product of the exploitation of animals."

"Oh. That sounds hard. Not sure what that implies."

"Really? I'm amazed. Well, you're right, it is hard, but don't worry. We'll educate you. It'll be fun. Here, have a look at this."

She flicked open her new 'Pulse and commanded :

"Show egg video."

She stared at the display. It wasn't a holo version so when the video started playing she sat next to me on the bed so that I could see. I breathed in her sweet scent and nearly fainted. It was hard to concentrate on the video with Mimi being so close. My body was quivering: she must have noticed but didn't say anything, instead describing what was happening on the screen. It was quite horrific.

"See these cute chicks? They're being separated out and placed into trays because they're males. They're no use in the process. They're being thrown into that hopper now. People show more respect for tennis balls. Look at them being chucked in. See, one's landed on the floor. But these are the lucky ones. The hopper is a gas chamber. They pick out the bodies and send them on as food for reptiles and birds. And look here, Michael. These are the unfortunate ones: straight into the macerator."

"Eh?"

"The grinder. They are ground alive. Forty million or more treated this way in this country alone. It makes me sick. Well?"

"I don't know what to say. I've never actually thought about what I'm eating to be honest, Mimi. I'm quite shocked by that. Eating an egg or a chicken will never be the same again."

"Precisely. This is no way to treat another conscious being. And I haven't started you on the dairy industry yet. And as for pigs, Michael, they're probably more intelligent than your mother."

Oh, and she laughed.

What a wonderful sound.

"Well, that I can believe," I said, chuckling.

"Don't worry, though, Michael. We'll go easy on you. It'll be good, honest."

"OK, I'll go with it."

"Great. Well, I'd better be going then or I'm going to miss my lecture. Thursday, then, about 7. Look, here's the address and my new number. I'm on the other side of the river, out towards the sports stadium."

"OK, look forward to it."

She stood and made her own way towards the front door, confident and serene, smiling at me as she left and ruffling Willow a good-bye.

I stood transfixed as she turned off down the street towards St. Peter's and the city beyond, overwhelmed with a joy that even the absence of a good-bye peck on the cheek could not diminish. I continued standing there, rooted by hopeful thoughts, for how long I know not, until Willow batted me forcefully on the leg, as if to say: "Oi! I'm still here."

"Well, well, Willow. That was unexpected."

And, to celebrate, we went off for a game of footie at the rec.

◆ ◆ ◆

It was tempting to link Mimi's visit to the feeling that I'd experienced at St. Peter's - that God would agree to help me win her affections if I decided to be active in the Cause.

So there is a God. And he listens.

But what now? If I was to keep my side of the bargain then I would likely end up dead. What use would Mimi's affection be then?

The question became more than hypothetical when Seth returned home later that day. He barged untypically unceremoniously into my room, startling Willow, who barked loudly in alarm.

"Jaz wants to see you tomorrow. Same place. At 4," he said coldly.

"Eh? What about? What?"

"Just be there, Michael, he's expecting you."

Humongous anticlimax.

29 THE RESCUE

Father Cuthbert tried to calm and compose his raging mind. He decided to go through it all one more time. It had been quite a while ago but the Bishop would not drop the case.

Had he done anything wrong? Had there been indecent intent? He couldn't find it, either in his motivation or in his actions.

A young man who he didn't know had approached him, wanting to speak about something or other. The youth had looked troubled and Father Cuthbert welcomed him with a smile. Before they had started talking, Father Cuthbert had seen a small boy, running at speed. The boy tripped and fell, banging his chin on the ground.

Yes, that was all true: Father Cuthbert was sure.

Now, slow it down.

Instinctively, Father Cuthbert had rushed forward to help the stricken boy. He reacted faster than anyone else and reached the boy first. The boy lay prostrate and had begun to cry and scream.

So far, all correct. What next, then? Slow now, be sure. Control the breath.

Father Cuthbert had placed his left hand under the boy's chest, lifting him slightly onto his left side so that the boy was facing him, then reached with his right arm to cup under the boy's left shoulder. Then, decisively and with a flourish, he scooped the boy upwards, nimbly rising to his feet himself as he did so. The inertia of the move brought the boy – who must have been no more than five or six years old – swinging in towards Father Cuthbert's torso. Father Cuthbert removed his arm from under the boy's shoulder and swept it under his bottom, supporting him.

Where had my hand rested? Think, think.

His right hand had been resting along the boy's hip or side, alongside his kidneys perhaps, but certainly not on the cheeks of his bottom. It was Father Cuthbert's forearm that was providing the support for the boy's weight.

And then? What happened then?

The boy was still screaming.

"There, there. It's alright little fella, let's see what you've hurt shall we?"

Father Cuthbert could remember that exactly; those were definitely the words he had used, spoken in a smooth, kind tone.

He had moved his other hand, which had been supporting the boy's back, and cupped the back of his head. He had pressed on it carefully, lowering it to cushion softly on his own shoulder. The screaming had subsided to sobbing. Father Cuthbert gently kissed the boy's head.

Then the shock, the memory of which jolted Father Cuthbert physically and disrupted his controlled breathing.

"Leave my son alone. Pervert!"

A loud, cackling voice thundered across the tendons of the past, startling him even now with its vehemence as it reverberated in the small room, causing the yukka to tremble. He hadn't been given time to respond. Father Cuthbert, kneeling in meditation, was hit by a painful physical sensation like a slap whiplashing through time. It rocked him on his knees as his mind replayed the incident of the boy being snatched from his grasp. The sound of the boy's wailing continued to reverberate around the small room.

And now? Emptiness...

Father Cuthbert had stood transfixed, baffled into silence and immobility. A swarm formed around the woman who he presumed was the mother, shoving him brusquely aside as they moved in unison down the church steps towards the street. He never saw them again.

He had continued standing there, confused and uncertain as to what to do, as the other parishioners slowly dispersed. The young man that he had been speaking to had vanished. One of the last parishioners to leave, a gaunt elderly lady, was the only one to acknowledge his presence, breaking the spell of his bemusement.

"Thank you, Father. A lovely service, as usual. See you next Sunday."

She touched him lightly on the elbow and walked away. That was the last friendly gesture that he would remember as a priest.

So, that was it. I am certain. All of the events. All of the intentions.

There had been no wrongdoing on his part, neither in thought nor action. He had rushed to help the boy and comfort him, the only motive being that of pure love for another being.

Father Cuthbert's breathing was regular and very serene. With his eyes still closed he sensed the yukka plant and reached out to its energy. Peace enveloped him, soft as cashmere.

He let his mind review the aftermath of the incident. Not long afterwards the Bishop had been on the phone – typical of the Church to hold on to such an outmoded form of communication – berating him for allowing himself to be accused of molesting a child.

Berating him! Father Cuthbert dwelt on that momentarily, following the entrails of the action, trying to understand why the

Bishop's initial reaction had been one of accusation rather than enquiry or support.

Let the past flow by and learn its lessons. Breathe in. See the way the pieces move, understand their strategies. Breathe out.

It was clear. The Bishop did not like him, disapproved of his running of the parish, his sermons, his overtures to the other communities in the city. All he had needed was half an excuse to push him out. And now he had it. Accused of molesting a young boy. Kissing a boy and caressing his bottom. Father Cuthbert involuntarily chuckled quietly at the absurdity of it, but he recognised that there was no way back. The mothers and a certain Mrs. Smith had been adamant that their version of events was accurate. The investigation had proceeded slowly but no witnesses had come forward in his defence. He had appealed – twice – but there was no way of demonstrating his innocence when the Bishop – judge and jury – was already considering the punitive sentence. At best he would leave the parish; be appointed somewhere where the notoriety that the Bishop was about to rake up for him would not matter greatly. Some remote location overseas, no doubt. At worst, he would be ostracised and excommunicated.

Excommunicated.

Excommunicated from what? Some man-made concoction of spirituality whose experience could not match the surge of elation and emotion he experienced by communing deeply with other beings and nature.

Father Cuthbert was no longer troubled. He had thoroughly examined both his intentions and his actions and now drew spiritual strength from the conviction that both were pure.

He allowed himself to remain swaddled by his meditative state a while longer, encapsulated by the energy surges of the yukka, revelling in the eddies buffeting small particles of dust, absorbing the warmth of the light that filled the room.

Peace. Pure joy.

As he slowly transitioned from his deep self-examination, Father Cuthbert became aware of an insistent scratching sound at the front door of the presbytery. He arose, wobbling slightly from the stiffness in his knees and hips, stretched himself straight and plodded unsteadily to investigate. His limbs may have felt stiff and difficult to move but he felt an energy, peace and lightness of spirit that only comes with the perfect knowledge that he was at one with the universe.

The scratching intensified. Father Cuthbert was surprised that he could not see a silhouette beyond the frosted window pane of the door. He hesitated but the scratching sounded desperate.

He opened the door. A dog sat by the entrance, quiet now, gazing up into his eyes with anticipation.

"Hello, Mullet, what are you doing here?"

Mullet cocked her head to one side, one ear pointing straight up, the other flopped down. She looked comical. She stood and turned, then took a few paces towards the entrance gate before pausing and looking back quizzically over her shoulder at Father Cuthbert.

"Let me get my coat then."

Paltry preparations complete, Father Cuthbert stepped over the threshold of the presbytery door, closing it firmly behind him, then followed Mullet out through the gate.

St. Peter watched them go, his bells tolling frantically and furiously, but Father Cuthbert's focus lay straight ahead.

Beyond, the street and the city beckoned.

30 THE EPIPHANY

My first epiphany occurred on the day that Michael took us back to the fetid pool at the far end of the city park. We hadn't been there since we had first met; in fact we hadn't even gone in the castle park: it was well away from our normal routine.

Michael was unusually quiet that day. He'd normally jabber on to me about something or other as we were walking but his aura was confused, as well as a little subdued: he walked in silence, slightly stooped.

When we arrived at the pool, I sensed an angry presence and started growling. A man soon stepped out from some bushes where he'd been hiding. I didn't like him and barked furiously. He had a very turbulent, disturbed aura and smelled of angst. Michael didn't appear to notice anything untoward about him though, and spoke to me rather roughly:

"Shut up and sit still."

I acquiesced. It was very warm so, notwithstanding the anxiety in the air, when the pair of them started to chat I lay down and dozed, not really listening but using the soft vibrations of their whispered voices like a lullaby, trying to calm myself down. I allowed myself to fall asleep.

The evil man and his presence had already vanished when Michael roused me and encouraged me to move on. Michael was still depressed as we walked through the park towards the centre of the city. We were well away from any roads and he let me scamper about off-lead. I tried to cheer him up by jumping and knocking the football out of his hands but he refused to kick it for me and said, dully:

"Not now, Willow. Please."

He was clearly jaded and, after a short while of plodding along listlessly, and while we were still a long way from the castle, he flopped down on the grass.

"Let's lie here awhile, Willow, drink in the blue."

He lay on his back and closed his eyes, using his folded up top as a pillow. I'd already dozed by the pool and was wide awake but snuggled up to him for comfort. The warmth of the late afternoon sun on my skin was relaxing and I too rolled onto my back, flank up against Michael, paws up in the air. A slightly undignified pose, perhaps, but very comfortable nevertheless.

Relaxed, relaxed, I meshed my breathing with Michael's and stared up at the sky. Everything was tranquil. There were few people in the park, certainly at this hour and this far out from the centre. There was no wind to carry traffic noise, only an occasional wisp of soft breeze to tickle the hairs on my muzzle. Then, just as Michael had said, I breathed in the blue of the sky, felt it in my lungs, passing into my blood, coursing through my body. And then I breathed it back out again, there, just there in front of me, all in time with Michael…

…

nowhere to focus on the blue firmament

…

so I gaze beyond

…

swarm into the space beyond the sky

…

from my vantage point I look down at the earth

...

splendiferous beauty makes me gasp in awe

...

countless molecules sucked in by the partial vacuum

...

my muscles have created in my lungs

...

gush through membranes and into my blood stream

...

course through my body

...

create energy in wondrous chemical reactions

...

others join the flow and are forced out

...

as the muscles contract

...

out into the near-still air of the park

...

are caught by eddies and they're off

...

hither thither are sucked into Michael's lungs

...

yes these the same molecules

...

that were just within my own body

...

then out again

...

into the bees into the cats into the rats

...

off they wander in a long random dance

...

here they engage in reaction

...

are transformed

...

there they coalesce

...

are transformed

...

are never the same

...

never the same

...

and yet they are the same

...

the same molecules the same atoms

...

on they go tirelessly

...

until even the sun tires and dies

...

and they are engulfed by its expansion

...

and then they surf

...

surf the energy of the dying sun

…

then I but I am no longer that I

…

join them

…

or my molecules or my atoms or my energy joins them

…

on that wave

…

that wave flowing out

…

as the sun's death knell blows us on a majestic breaker

…

out into the depths of space

…

out

…

out

…

way beyond the blue sky I lie beneath

…

and we continue surfing

…

surfing

…

coasting

…

coasting

…

I dare to look back but there is no longer any earth

…

no longer any sun

…

just us atoms us particles us waves us energy

…

whizzing

…

whizzing along

…

and then we get caught

…

distracted by some gravity

…

and so we veer and we joy at the sensation

…

and we spin and we twirl

…

and in our excitement we join together

…

and we are molecules

…

and we play and we dance with other molecules

…

and then perhaps on a sunny day

…

far far away in another constellation

…

another galaxy

…

another universe

…

we are breathed in again

…

absorbed

…

momentarily trapped

…

and we wake

…

I breathed in and glanced at Michael, who was beginning to stir. Was that really Michael? Was that really the city beyond? The planet? Or were they all just a collection of trapped waves, particles, atoms, molecules, temporarily caught by wondrous forces, soon to be dissolved, ready to joyously surf amongst the galaxies once more?

In this form we exist no more than a micro breath of the universe.

I looked at the blue sky, the trees, the daisies, the insects milling about and felt a sense of utter peace like I had never experienced before. I felt light, weightless even, able to float at will amongst the startled populace should I have wished.

Here I am, this small dog in this small city on this small planet in this small solar system. Here I am, looking out, out beyond the stars. Only I know that I am not so small. I am of the fabric of the universe. I am of its essence. So insignificant and yet so vital. Me, us, all of us. We are all of its life, we are all of its essence.

And then, supremely confident and full of joy, I looked at Michael again, saw his subdued aura, and I knew with absolute certainty that the only thing – *the only thing!* – that matters whilst in this state is to assist fellow energies, captured in their own maelstroms of force, by alleviating the angst that is often associated with the temporary inability to surf amongst the stars.

I breathed in again, pure matter of the universe firing my spirit, looked at Michael and I knew that somewhen he would be my joyful companion surfer as we twirled through the miasma of wormholes into alternate dimensions. In the meantime, I gently placed my paw on his tum with a strength of feeling that I can only describe as love, and I delighted in the ecstasy of comfort when he lifted up his arm and ruffled my ears.

31 A MISSION

The air around the pool was humid and heavy when Willow and I arrived. The autumn day had been hot and in that sheltered, secluded spot the trees ruled over the breeze, trapping the air, rendering it fetid.

It felt oppressive, or was that a reflection of my mood? I had struggled to form coherent, continuous thoughts since the previous afternoon. Either event was momentous on its own – Mimi's visit and Seth's announcement – and in combination the two proved more than my mind could bear. I had struggled to sleep. If I tried focussing on Mimi then Jaz would blunder into that serene space, whereas her image was responsible for preventing any structured, rational thought on the consequences of what I anticipated that Jaz might say.

Am I worrying about nothing? It might only be an update from Jaz, not any serious task setting.

I didn't have long to wait alone by the pool. Willow had been growling and I'd only just settled him down by my feet when a figure approached – unexpectedly – from some bushes beyond the far side of the pool. The man startled us both and Willow began barking defensively.

"Shut up and sit still."

He laid back at my feet and curled up small.

"Michael," said the man. Half question, half statement.

"Yes," hesitatingly.

"Man, things have changed. Gotta move fast. Jaz's been taken."

"What?"

"He's gone, man. The spols got him. 's OK though, it'll take them awhile to catch up with us."

"Us?"

The man ignored my perplexity and said again:

"We've gotta move fast. Tomorrow afternoon. There's a fascist rally in the city. Infiltrate it. Be there no later than 3. Here…"

He handed me a thin tube like an elongated bullet. It was smooth, shiny and felt warm to the touch.

"This is the device, man. Use it like a suppository."

"Like a what?"

"Shit, man, a suppository." And then he laughed, guffawed loudly even, before recollecting himself, realising that no-one must know that we were here. "You stick it up your arse." And he chuckled again, more quietly this time.

He must have sensed how baffled I was, because he calmed himself down and explained some more:

"It's the latest development, man. Impossible to trace once it's inside the body. And with a kill-radius of ten yards. Easy to use. Just insert it, be there on time and we detonate it remotely. It'll be quite a spectacle."

"Uh?"

"Don't worry, man, you won't feel a thing. It'll be instant and it won't even be you who sets it off, so there's less of that anxiety factor. All you have to do is focus on the place and the time, then relax."

"Relax?"

Is he insane?

"Is this thing dangerous? And anyway, who the hell are you? I've never seen you before."

"'course you haven't. It's inadvisable to know too many people. Do you think I'd be here if Jaz knew me well? The less we know the better, man. All you need to know is the time and the place. Your destiny is assured, man, you'll be a great hero."

"I don't want to be a hero."

"No, but you wanna do what's right, don't you, man? Anyway, too late for that now. We know that you shook on an agreement with Jaz."

"And what if I change my mind?"

"Not possible, man. There's no way back in this game. You either help the Cause or die an undignified death that no-one will remember. That's the choice."

I hesitated, unsure of what to say or do. I was petrified.

"Are you threatening me?" I blurted, eventually.

He blanked my question. "3pm tomorrow. The rally. Insert the device about an hour before. Good luck, man, you're doing a great thing."

With these words he scarpered, rushing back round the pool to the far side, disappearing into the undergrowth.

I stood there for a long time, stock-still, stunned.

Eventually I became aware that, of course, I was not alone. Willow had relaxed and was lying down, snuggled up against my feet. That touch brought me gradually round to reality. After a few more minutes the leaden feeling that was anchoring me to the spot abated, allowing me to move.

I pocketed the device and wandered off slowly back through the park in the direction of home. My legs felt heavy, difficult to move, my body lethargic and weary, burdened by troublesome thoughts.

Willow must have sensed my downbeat mood. He jumped up and head-butted the ball from my arms, then stood there teasing me, front paws flat to the grass, rump up and his tail wagging furiously.

"Let's play football!" his whole body screamed excitedly.

"Not now, Willow. Please."

I stumbled a few steps further forward and then collapsed heavily onto the ground, trampled down by the weight of the atmosphere. The grass felt cool, a welcome sensation pushing through the maelstrom of turmoil on that sultry afternoon. I lay on my back, rested my head on my sweater and looked up at the sky.

"Let's lie here awhile, Willow, drink in the blue."

I closed my eyes and tried to regulate my ragged breathing. It was the stress: my stomach felt churned up and queasy. Willow snuggled up to me: his presence and touch were a great comfort.

Threads sparkled to life in my mind, elongated and coalesced into coherent thought.

What to do? There is no painless option. Run away? Confess all to Mimi, persuade her to elope with me, disappear forever.

As if that could happen!

I'd been disappointed by Mimi before, didn't have the confidence that this was it, that she was finally ready to go with me. And, it was a near certainty that the cell would catch up with me. If not them, the spols. The cell would kill me, would the spols? It was rumoured that people were disappearing, taken in the night for questioning, never returning, even deleted from social media and the net. Mothers and friends shouting their protest were just a low whisper lost in the gale of Government hyperbole.

So: run like a coward?

A coward.

That thought again. Had I, in fact, not been running and hiding all my life? Run like a coward and, most likely, die. And die for what? Nothing to show. A failure. A total failure.

So was the option to go ahead with the wishes of the cell? I was in no doubt that the device would kill me, along with many others.

But how could I kill others? I'd always thought of myself as a peaceful person, opposed to killing and violence in general. Was I actually capable of murdering another person? But I wouldn't be doing the killing, would I? The other sleeper had said that the device would be operated remotely, not by me. I was simply the conduit, joining in with a demo, unaware of anything even to the end.

That was a naive way of looking at it, surely. I had the device. Why not throw it in the river? Await my fate, the only casualty being me, the victim of my own stupidity. Was that not the bravest thing to do? Or hand the device in to the spols, admit everything.

What a betrayal of the Cause that would be! And, at best, I'll end up behind bars for years, if not for life. Nothing positive will be gained in either scenario. And, in losing me, a force for good will be lost. The world will be poorer as a result.

A force for good? A force for good as an instrument of death and destruction? How could that be? But was that not the rationale for all wars? Soldiers are the instruments of good. That was a rationale I'd always rejected. How could killing be good? The end justifies the means: another adage I'd always dismissed as trite.

I was trapped. To die in vain, knowing that I'd not harmed anyone else, yet not advancing the Cause I believed in, and the world losing a force for good. To kill others, anathema to me, yet knowing that those others are full of bad thoughts, are a force for evil.

Round and round they go, my thoughts, spiralling ever outwards out of control. What to do?

One thing seemed certain: I would not be around on the planet much longer. The only question was how I was to say good-bye to my fellow eight and a half billion humans.

Eight and a half billion!

How many?

How could losing a few be so significant, particularly if they were bad people?

Round and round they go, my thoughts, colliding randomly into each other, mental Brownian motion failing to resolve itself into an answer.

What to do?

I became aware of Willow's touch, his pressure against my side. The sensation felt like the touch of water on parched tongue to a dehydrated desert traveller. Breaking through my troubled thoughts, it made me wonder how this creature, so much smaller and so different to me, and professedly much less intelligent, could be such a friend and such a comfort to somebody like myself. He was much more so indeed than any of the other eight and a half billion humans on this planet.

Eight and a half billion!

Eight and a half billion people. And, by all accounts, continuing to grow at an increasing rate. How could this beautiful, fragile planet tolerate such numbers? All wanting food, all wanting shelter, all wanting a comfortable standard of living. And the food! As Mimi had recently explained to me, imagine the suffering caused by feeding all of these people to the standards that they aspire to.

Eight and a half billion!

Too many, surely. And so – and then the thought did crystallize, grow and remain in my mind – how could it possibly be wrong to remove some of the bad people? The people the Cause was targeting were certainly bad – I was sure of that. These were people who not only expressed hatred towards others but inflicted violence on them with bile and venom. They were proud of it too, and boasted about it within their own circle: no qualms, no remorse. Unbridled evil.

So how could it be wrong to remove these people from an overcrowded planet? Would the planet miss them amongst the other eight and a half billion?

I don't think so.

To kill them must therefore be a good thing.

I opened my eyes slowly and looked at the sky, dimming now from its deep blue as the sun lowered in the horizon. The moon, though still faint, had already made its appearance. Vapour trails from a couple of aeroplanes marked the sky, converging straight lines that seemed to point at the moon. I tried to imagine myself riding those trails like a road, escaping off this madhouse planet towards some finer place.

But the journey was too hard. I couldn't focus and solve the problems. I lacked the mental fortitude and wilted even as I sensed the atmosphere thin and space grow darker before me. I panicked and my thoughts fell back down to the mundane earth.

The thoughts, or rather the terrible thought, was still there, glowing, burning bright, searing in its intensity.

How can it be anything but good to remove bad from the world?

Repeated, again and again.

Once more that presence, that loving touch. I disconnected from my thoughts and ruffled Willow's ears, but when I turned to look at him the image was blurred by tears.

PART 4
DENOUEMENT

32 THE CITY AND THE STREET

Ah.

You've stayed until the end: well done.

And now do you understand? Can you see clearly now?

What do you mean, you're still a little confused?

How can you not see what's in front of you?

You must know this city: it's *your* city.

And this street? You must know it: why, it's *your* street.

But wait.

Hold on.

Look there.

Look!

See, down there in the street, that person leaving the house in a hurry. Yes, you see them now. Wait: hold on a minute.

That's… that's…

That person… it's *you*, isn't it?

33 THE CHASE

After the trip to the fetid pool Michael's aura had changed worryingly, tending to pulse red from an ochre base. I sensed that he was anxious and angry: our rest in the park had done nothing to alleviate his mood.

I, on the contrary, felt super-charged; buoyed up from surfing the galaxies. The experience still felt so real, even now that my paws were clearly firmly back on solid earth. Even so, my energy was unable to shake off Michael's angst. I was jocular, I was playful, I used all of my cute-dog looks and poses but all it achieved was half-hearted soft ruffling of my fur and some cuddles in return. I sensed the love that he felt for me but also that he was deeply troubled.

Michael had an uneasy night. He tossed and turned. Any sleep would have been fitful, not restful. Nevertheless, he adopted our normal week-end morning routine: let me out for a quick pee in the back yard before going back to bed for an hour or so. He followed up with more of the usual: off to the rec for a game of footie. We played, ostensibly normally, but I could detect that his heart was not in it. His mind was preoccupied; his aura stormy.

It was after lunch that the break from routine came. Instead of studying whilst listening to music – a prelude to more footie at the rec – he lay down on his bed and closed his eyes. His breathing was ragged and I could both sense and see how he was trying hard to regulate it. I placed my paw sympathetically on the bed, close to his chest.

"It's alright, Willow, I'll be alright," was all he could muster.

I jumped up onto the bed and snuggled up close, hoping to ease his troubles.

♦ ♦ ♦

Oh my God! I have to make a move. Fast!

The rally moved off at 3. That was the ordained time. I had to be at the right place or it would be disastrous.

How could I have dozed off?

I'd hoped to have already left the house but I'd had a bad night's sleep and Willow's snuggle had relaxed me too much.

I juggled times in my mind. Distance. Time to walk. Time to jog. Time to run. How fit was I anyway? Would it arouse suspicion to run towards the field where they were gathering?

No. Yes.

I checked the bus's position on my 'Pulse and decided that I was going to have to catch it: timewise it was probably less risky than travelling on foot.

Bugger! No time to lose.

But first, the most difficult part. I was going to have to say goodbye to Willow. It was that thought alone that was destroying me inside. It felt as if my innards were being eaten by some monster, like in that gory film from the last century. I was going to have to barricade him in the bedroom to prevent him from following me. I could tell that he sensed that something was awry and knew what a determined dog he was.

Luckily Seth and my other house mate always went off to football on Saturday afternoons. I checked that they'd already left the house.

All good then.

I grabbed the broom from the kitchen.

First time it will have been used.

In preparation for Willow's incarceration I propped the broom against the wall outside the bedroom door. Then, so as to be ready to leave as soon as he was shut in, I went to the loo to implant the device. It was easier than I'd feared and any sensation of it residing within me faded quickly. It was done.

No going back now.

I could postpone the terrible deed no longer.

"Willow, stay. Stay!"

I held my hand up in a 'stop' sign.

"Stay!" Said forcefully. "Someone will come to fetch you very soon, I promise. I love you very much, little fella. I'm sorry that I have to leave."

I closed the door, tears streaming copiously down my face, leaving Willow in the room.

"Stay," I blubbed once more through the closed door, and jammed the broomstick between the handle and the door so that Willow could not open it from the inside.

"Goodbye, Willow, I love you so very much."

I stepped away, trying not to make a sound, but heard Willow beginning to scrabble, trying to open the door. He barked when he realised that it was stuck and started scratching and rattling the door violently.

I verified that the broom handle was secure.

"Stay!" I said firmly and left the house, shutting the door quietly behind me, biting my tongue in an effort to control my sobbing as I hurried down the street.

I turned the corner past St. Peter's and slowed, clearing my eyes of tears. I looked back down the street, allowed myself a few seconds of wallowing in happy memories, until persistent thoughts of Willow brought a lump to my throat.

Concentrate now, control your thoughts, blinker yourself to everything except what must be done.

There were two more vital things to do before heading onwards. First, I posted the letter that I'd written to Mimi the previous evening, confessing my love for her, explaining the predicament I was in and apologising for letting her down. Finally, no matter how much of the now precious time that it took, I slowed, flipped open my 'Pulse and texted her: '*URGENT! Have to vamoose! Please look after Willow 4 me. Much love. M x.*' Then I immediately switched it to flight mode to prevent any incoming messages or calls from distracting me.

Speeding up again, I turned the corner onto the main avenue leading into the city centre and reached the bus stop. The sign confirmed that the next bus was 3 minutes away.

14:35 now. Should be OK. Just.

◆ ◆ ◆

I was astonished when I realised that Michael was locking me in the bedroom. I'd known that his aura was all askew and should have been more proactive in helping him.

I tried opening the handle, the same as I'd done that very first day when he'd left me, but it wouldn't budge. I jumped up again and again, bashing it strongly with my paws: no use.

I barked wildly in anger and frustration.

"Stay!" I heard Michael say one more time from beyond the door.

What's going on?

I ran to the window. Michael was leaving in a hurry, jogging towards St. Peter's. I pawed at the window to no avail. There was no way to get past that obstacle without seriously injuring myself.

Back to the door: perhaps if I persisted in flipping the handle then whatever was jamming it would eventually give way. I tried and tried, my attempts becoming more frantic. No luck.

Where is Michael going in such a rush?

His angry aura did not augur well and filled me with foreboding. Anxiety turned to panic: my panting became ragged with the stress of the situation.

I tried the door handle again: what else was there to do? Still no good. I tried running straight at the door and bashing into it at speed but all that happened was that I hurt myself. Scratch, scratch, scratching did nothing useful. It would take hours to gouge and bite my way through and I sensed I didn't have that much time.

Flashbacks of my ordeal in the wheelie bin swept through me.

Trapped!

I was trapped. Dread and nausea coursed through my body. I vomited the contents of lunch into the corner, feeling slightly giddy. Exhaustion crushed me so that I lay spread-eagled on the floor, even though it couldn't have been more than a few minutes since Michael had left.

And then the answer came to me. It had worked in the wheelie bin and it was the only thing that I could do.

Suffused with defiant, universal energy, I began a violent assault on the handle and on the door, without concern for my physical well being, barking furiously at the same time. I had sustained this onslaught for perhaps only thirty seconds or so when, like on that miraculous occasion in the bin, I felt an unexpected impact on my muzzle and was sent careering backwards.

The door had opened.

"What the flippin' bell is going on in here?"

Seth!

Seth had returned home for some reason and opened the bedroom door. Not only that but, confronted by the racket I was making, he had also left the front door ajar.

I scarpered out of there before he'd had a chance to consider what to do. By the time that Seth had recovered his composure and looked down the street, I had already turned past St. Peter's and was racing towards the main avenue, following Michael's unmistakeable aural and scent trails. I turned the corner into the avenue, running hard towards the city centre.

There!

A hundred yards ahead, Michael was boarding a bus!

♦ ♦ ♦

14:38, so where's the bus? Ah, here it comes. OK. Let's say fifteen minutes for the 3 miles to the convening square. It should be enough time but it's tight.

The stress cramped my stomach again, made me feel queasy. Worrying about the time was not something that I'd anticipated.

How stupid of me – normally such a compulsive, punctilious, punctual individual to the point of being irritating to others - to get into this situation.

The bus drew to a halt and the entrance doors swirled open. As I was boarding, I cast a glance to the right. There, in the distance!

Willow. How come? Shit!

There was no-one queuing behind me so the doors closed as soon as I'd jumped on. I tapped my destination into the ticket machine, scanned my 'Pulse and pushed my way to the back. The bus was crowded. I was glared and cursed at as I edged my way up the aisle but I desperately needed to confirm if that had really been Willow in the distance or just a similar looking dog.

"Please. Please. 'scuse me," I muttered as I trod and elbowed my way up to the rear. Dignified it was not. The back seat was fully occupied and I had to strain on tiptoe to see out. It was sufficient. My world shattered. My mind, already in turmoil, was now sent careering out of control. Not only was it Willow, but he was sprinting faster than I'd ever known, stretching his body out in great leaps and bounding forward vigorously.

What if he catches up? Oh, God. No!

The bus was accelerating towards the main feeder road into the centre and appeared to be gaining on Willow: he must have been fifty yards or so behind.

We are moving fast and smoothly. We'll be OK at this speed.

I ran the route through in my mind, trying to picture the locations of bus stops, guestimating the number of passengers boarding and leaving at those places on a Saturday. Then I processed the model in my head: Willow against the bus.

Surely he can never keep up that manic speed over distance. Can he?

My computation suggested that the bus would outrun Willow provided the stops near the shops were not too prolonged. I drew comfort from the fact that at this time of day the shoppers would already be disgorging cash and not yet ready to leave.

Then why is the bus so busy?

With Willow trailing, I relaxed a little, drawing breath and regulating my mind. In doing so I was able to take notice of my fellow passengers for the first time since boarding. Predominantly male, most had painted their faces and heads blue. Their clothes were shredded by design. But, most of all I was struck by their stance, their expressions and the hate in their eyes. Blueheads headed for the rally: I was in a bus full of fascists.

Bastards! Perhaps it won't matter if I am late. Get the buggers right here.

But what about the driver? And any others who had nothing to do with the rally, pure innocents?

There are no innocents, Seth believes.

Even if he was right, there might have been people on the bus who were sympathetic to the Cause. It was best to keep to the original plan.

Oh, oh, we're slowing down. Traffic lights turning to red.

Anxiety slapped me again. I rose up on tip toe, virtually doing a chin-up on the bus's support bar, straining to get a view out of the back window. Nothing. No sign of Willow. I flopped back down onto my heels and waited impatiently for the lights to change, counting the seconds.

Get on with it. Finally. Green.

I stretched up again as the driver moved off.

Rats!

Willow was merely a few yards away and running as tirelessly as before.

Unbelievable! How can he keep this pace up?

The bus turned right and accelerated down the straight road. I lost my balance in the manoeuvre and went sprawling, landing on someone's lap on the opposite side of the aisle.

"Oi! Calm yourself down, mate. Just keep still. Wazzack! Get off."

"Sorry."

As I hauled myself up I caught a glimpse of Willow running on the pavement beside the bus. Amazingly, he had caught up and was dodging pedestrians at breakneck speed. I fought away feelings of panic as the bus continued to accelerate. We outpaced Willow and he dropped behind. I checked the time: 14:43.

It's mainly a straight run now. Looking good for 3pm!

◆ ◆ ◆

I was infused with a universal force and ran like a cheetah giving chase. No, I was better than the cheetah because there was no abating my speed. The bus sped away and gained on me down the arterial road towards the city, but it then had to stop at traffic lights and I caught up, running alongside as it turned right towards the centre.

I saw Michael briefly. He was peering out of the window, looking surprised and concerned. My greatest certainty at that point was that I must catch up with him: I knew that he needed me.

A bus stop in the distance.

Problem solved: the bus would slow, the doors open and we would be reunited. Michael's peculiar behaviour back at the house was surely an aberration caused by whatever was troubling him. A simple misunderstanding: he would be delighted to see me, I was sure.

But the bus didn't stop. I was incredulous.

Surely Michael would have pressed the stop button!

He had seen me. I had noticed the recognition in his face, even though it had only been a momentary glimpse. Why, then, would he not get off the bus? In my certainty that it would stop, I had slowed, and it was now gaining on me rapidly.

I decided that this wasn't the time for questioning or analytical musing and simply accelerated again, bounding forward with renewed vigour. The bus was now on the wide multi-lane highway that skirted the centre and quickly raced away from me despite my efforts.

Undeterred, I sprinted on, guided now only by Michael's strong emotional pull.

♦ ♦ ♦

Willow was out of sight. There was only light traffic on the ring road and the bus was making good progress.

14:48.

Surely, Willow could not catch up now. We'd be arriving near the rally in less than ten minutes. Then there wouldn't be long to wait before the appointed time. Even if he was able to trace the bus's route, would Willow arrive in time? And how would he find me in the large crowd that was anticipated for the rally?

He might not find me but still be hurt by the explosion. The big problem is that he always seems to know where I am. This is terrifying!

The thought of harming Willow, who had brought so much comfort to my life, was too much to bear. I desperately tried to recalculate distances and speed as best as I could. Willow should certainly be slowing down. He wasn't used to long runs, let alone long sprints. My mental maths did not help in relieving my tension: the sums were approximate, clearly, but, unless he faded, put Willow at the convening ground at around 3pm.

Too close for comfort!

I searched frantically for a solution but couldn't think of any that I was happy with. I briefly considered getting off the bus whilst still near the centre, where I could run to a different target. The only plausible one that came to mind – thanks to Mimi – was the university department where it was known that they did or funded experiments on live animals. But I wasn't familiar with the layout of the building and certainly didn't have time to research it. More significantly, I didn't have control of the device's timing and it was probable that Willow would simply run me down. That was the worst of all possible outcomes.

No. Distance is the only answer. Stay on the bus, hope for no more delays and that Willow tires and slows.

Fate, though, was not on my side that day.

We were rolling well until we'd finished skirting the pedestrian shopping area. The bus then turned into the road leading away from the centre. From here it was only another mile or so.

Tantalisingly close.

Suddenly we just stopped, nowhere near a junction or traffic lights. I couldn't see the road ahead because of the crush of people on the bus, but cars in the adjacent lane had also stopped. Frustrated, I rechecked the time: 14:50.

If I leave now, there's enough time to run the remaining distance.

But no-one else on the bus shifted and indecision left me anchored to the spot. Stressed and uncertain, I strained to peer out of the back window: no sign of Willow. I counted an andante beat, willing the bus to move, stomach churning, to no avail.

14:52. Shit!

An aeon passed. Eventually there was some slight movement forwards, perhaps one or two cars' lengths, then we stopped again.

Despairing now, I abandoned my scruples. "What's going on, do you know?" I asked a bluehead standing further down the bus whose eye I happened to catch. He shrugged his shoulders but reached further forward a couple of seats and tapped someone on the shoulder, a friend perhaps, who did the same thing in turn. A message quickly filtered back:

"Looks like they've closed the road ahead because the rally's about to start. We might have to get off here and walk, or join half way."

Woa!

I checked the time again: 14:55. At this rate the explosion would happen on the bus – not what I wanted. My sphincter tightened with the tension. Just then the bus moved again, slowly, but instead of continuing forwards on its normal route, it turned left into a minor shopping street.

"This is it," said the bluehead. "We'll have to get off next stop and walk. He's come off his route. Who knows where we'll end up if we stay on."

Panic!

The bus lurched: someone had pinged for a stop. I strained to look out of the back as those sitting there stood up, getting ready to dismount. What I saw filled me with dread. Willow was rounding the corner, sprinting as vigorously as ever towards the bus.

♦ ♦ ♦

The bus gained steadily on me down the long avenue that skirted the pedestrian area. I sensed neurons firing doubts in my brain as I pounded the tarmac, running alongside the kerb, trying to make as much use of cars' slipstreams as possible. I easily squished any misgivings. This was the time for action, not for hypothetical debate. The one imperative drove me forward, powered my muscles, spurred them on to supercanine feats.

One imperative: must help Michael!

Why had I not understood the logical conclusion of his aura and acted on it sooner?

Not now, Willow, not now. The inquest can come later, now's the time to run.

Run!

Run.

Run!

I must have been half a mile behind when the bus turned off the avenue. The road was straight and I could see it clearly negotiating the curve. The traffic lights had been green: no luck for me there. I lost sight of it but was guided by the shifting vector of Michael's aural attraction. I continued my relentless sprint.

As I approached the junction I experienced a thrilling sensation. Michael's force was getting stronger with every stride. The bus must have slowed or even stopped. Excitement surged within me, enticing every atom into an orgiastic energy release as I careered around the corner.

There it is! A hundred yards - less than ten seconds - away, trapped in traffic.

I became weightless, shooting forward on a cushion of air.

As I was about to reach it, there was some movement ahead of the bus, allowing it to advance again. It turned left into a narrower street but I was moving with the fluidity of cheerful sunlight and caught up easily. And there was Michael, peering out of the back window.

No escaping me now.

I slowed, keeping pace with the bus, which soon came to a stop. Its doors opened and I seized my chance, jumping onto the back step.

Too eager!

A wave of people was flooding out and I felt a strong kick on my muzzle.

Too accurate to be an accident?

I was propelled backwards by the force of the impact and landed on the kerb with a thud, leaving me winded.

"Scram, mutt!" shouted a yob, perhaps the one who had hoofed me. Focussing intently despite the shock, I couldn't sense Michael amongst the descending passengers.

I see him now, still at the window. He's staying on.

Decisively, I jumped up and in two massive strides reached the open front door, which was totally clear as no-one was boarding. I leapt in, looked down the bus and saw Michael. He was looking directly at me and caught my eye.

At last. Reunited!

♦ ♦ ♦

Oh my God! I've been caught. Willow is right outside. I cannot let him be with me. This is a complete disaster. What to do? Oh my God.

Oh, oh: we're stopping. Blast. He's going to get on.

Eh? Shit! You bastard! You've kicked my best friend in the face. Bastard!

Willow had slumped into the gutter. The blueheads were piling off, blocking the exit. Indeed, most people on the bus were dismounting here, mainly thugs headed for the rally, leaving a few innocent stragglers on board.

What to do? What to do?

Willow recovered quickly and sprinted to the front of the bus.

Shit, he's on.

I had to get off; I simply couldn't allow him to be with me. Impulsively, I jumped out, just as the back door was closing. I stumbled onto the pavement, clattering into the last passenger to dismount. He cursed but I ignored him and turned back to face the bus. Willow's nose was pressed against the door. He was looking forlorn as the bus moved off again. I dared to glimpse at my 'Pulse: 14:58.

There was hardly enough time. Even if I could have made it to the rally, Willow would probably have caught up with me. And I had to get away from there: I did not want to kill innocents in the street.

But, most of all, I cannot kill Willow. I must distance myself from him!

Distance. Distance! How? How?

It came to me, as if revealed by heaven: the answer, the only way.

Lightened by certainty I sprinted with elemental fury back towards the centre of the city, turned right and, ignoring the insults of startled shoppers, headed straight for the shopping hub.

♦ ♦ ♦

What's going on? He saw me and then jumped off. He's avoiding me. But his aura is swirling tempestuously. I have to catch up with him, soothe away the pain.

The bus is moving, accelerating away from Michael. There's nothing else for it; I'm a master of these situations now. I know what to do.

Like a rabid lunatic dog I began barking furiously and launched myself repeatedly at the bus door, bouncing back with the impact, then growled menacingly at the few remaining passengers, exposing vicious, wicked fangs.

"Stop! Stop the bus! There's a wild dog up here. Stop now!" Several terrified passengers backed away from me, haranguing the driver. Alarmed, he hit the brakes, sending half of them careering forwards, falling onto their backs. I did a dummy growling lunge for them, snapping the air viciously, then ran back and restarted my attack on the back door.

"Open the door, you fool, he wants to get out!"

In a flash, I was on the pavement, running, following Michael's still strong aural attraction. He was headed for the centre. As soon as I rounded the corner, I saw him. I'd never seen him run so fast, but he'd be no match for me. I'd catch him in a matter of seconds.

But…

…then the world shifted on its axis, as if Atlas himself had stumbled.

I felt a field force knock me sideways, sending me tumbling over pedestrians' legs. I ended up lying flat on my side. But the shock wave had passed, allowing me to look up along the road towards Michael. He was still sprinting undeterred onto the bridge that led towards the castle and the shops.

At that moment, I knew that everything had changed, that nothing would be the same again. It might have been Michael's body running onto the bridge, but it was not Michael. His aura had completely vanished. The emotional force drawing me towards him had also disappeared.

As I watched, not even bothering to get up and resume the chase, I saw exactly the same thing as I'd done that day, all those weeks ago, when Jake lay dying. Michael's spirit swirled from his body, sensed its way back down the road towards me, enveloped me in a loving embrace, then rocketed upwards in swift departure.

I remained prostrate on the pavement, bereft and distraught, head between my paws, thunderstruck at such a calamitous fate. We had not known each other for long, certainly not as measured by rotations of the sun, but the bond between Michael and I was much more fundamental than anything temporal. And now he was gone.

Gone, even as his bodily husk sped towards the bridge.

♦ ♦ ♦

My senses heightened by tension, I rejoiced in the sound and feel of the air rushing past my ears as I sprinted towards the centre. I could feel – and my thoughts briefly stopped to wonder at how tactile the sensation was – Willow some way behind me. The awareness of his presence was so strong that I was able to clearly visualise the next few seconds and rejoiced in the certainty that, not only would he be safe, but that my solution to the crisis would result in no-one being hurt.

I'm on the bridge and there's only fifteen yards or so of running before I'm over the river. A matter of seconds.

Pumped up with joy I leapt onto the parapet without breaking stride, assisting my balance with the support of my hand, just to be sure. I stood, ignoring the shrieks of alarmed bystanders, glanced to my right, overjoyed to see Willow – at last exhausted by the chase – lying down on the pavement. Smiling, I jumped off and braced myself for impact with the water.

But I never felt it.

I hear the sweetest music playing. I recognise it immediately: it is my grandmother's music box. I remember it so well. Beautiful enamelled black, decorated with colourful flowers. And when you opened it, the ballerina inside would begin to dance, twirling gracefully to the crisp, clear notes of Swan Lake. She might only have been made of plastic but I loved her for her unparalleled, serene beauty. Then, as the clockwork mechanism wound down, the ballerina would slow.

I can see her now, faltering as the tempo drops and the notes, crisp and clear and shiny as stars in the darkest night

gently

fade

34 THE RESCUE

The nausea hit me like a volcanic eruption. My stomach heaved coincident with my legs buckling. I collapsed to the floor, landing on my knees, then bent over as my stomach churned and emptied its contents.

What an unexpected reaction!

The last spasm shook my body violently. Taking a shallow breath to avoid more retching, I re-read the text: '*URGENT! Have to vamoose! Please look after Willow 4 me. Much love. M x.*'

Vamoose? Urgent? What does he mean, vamoose? Look after Willow? How can he go away? Please, God, not now.

But why should my body have reacted in such a fashion to such simple words? It had been excessive, surely.

Very strange. But why then am I filled with a sense of dread?

Whatever the answer, I certainly could no longer deny to myself that I had fallen for Michael.

Shaking from the sickness, I tried phoning him, my voice juddering as I blurted out the number. There was no reply. I tried again: same result. Panicking now – and this new feeling also surprised me – I read out a text: *'Michael u alright? Where u going? Please reply. Love, Mimi xxx.'*

Right, girl, time to shift into action.

I cleared up the mess from the floor in a rush. Not the best job ever but, hey, my flatmates had gone off for the weekend so there was no need to be fastidious at that precise moment. I checked my 'Pulse: nothing back from Michael.

Grasp the nettle, girl, go for it.

There was only one thing to do. I simply left the house, running, determined to get to Michael's house to see if I could understand what was happening. My mind was spinning: it was impossible to hold on to a thread and follow it to a conclusion.

Why am I doing this, slobbering like a pubescent girl?

The streets were busy, full of people walking towards the centre. There were no buses to be seen. I suddenly remembered: it was the day of the rally and there were traffic restrictions in place. That explained the crowded pavements. I'd have to continue on foot but didn't have the fitness to run all of the way, so adopted a mix of jogging and walking. A hundred paces of each, counting them out, using the discipline as a kind of meditation, trying to control my thoughts and work out what was going on, not just with Michael but with my own feelings.

Michael had been chasing me since the early days of high school. I wasn't interested at first but he persevered and his image became etched in my mind as the school years ticked by. It wasn't an obsession or anything but, looking back on it now, I wonder whether part – *or was it all*? – of the reason I'd rejected other boys' advances was to remain available for him. But the silly boy would not make a move and even went and got himself a girlfriend, despite all my hints and poses.

That must have felt like a violent kick in the guts, that dancefloor rejection. Jeez, we were barely teens then. Come on, Michael, get over it!

Initially, university had been a shock to me: his presence at school had been pervasive but suddenly he was gone, vanished from my days. I struggled to adapt to his absence at first. Time and a light depression dulled the longing so that, by the time of the demo, his appearances in my mind were rare. In a trice, that chance meeting changed all that. Abruptly, inexplicably, I wanted him, as if all of the yearning and love he had felt for me over the years had suddenly crystallised in a reciprocal instant.

Michael was subdued on that day, made nervous by my continuous presence perhaps, but from the second we met I felt an affinity and closeness unparalleled in my life to date. The depression lifted. I was warm, I was happy, I was comfortable – because he was there, no other reason.

I was certain; it was him!

I was sure that we would start dating back in the city.

The trouble I went to in tracking him down after my 'Pulse was stolen! And now? The same thing again?

Just when it looked as if we might get together, he texts me and has to 'vamoose'. Vamoose! Such finality to the message, such a terrifying shock.

Lost to the physical world in thought, I barely registered consciously the fact that the crowds were thinning as I approached the centre. Then, as unexpectedly sudden as the nausea had been, I experienced another surge of sensation, like I'd been instantly swamped by a tidal wave of icy water. It caused me to snap out of my introspection. With surprise, I realised that I had become hyper-perceptive of my surroundings, as if I had somehow been boosted by a supernatural power. I was seeing, hearing, smelling and feeling everything in slow motion. The hairs all over my body stood on end;

my skin became a forest of goose-pimples. It was a sensation like I'd never experienced before: I could even compute my speed by calculating the cooling effect of the breeze on my face. I saw everything, heard everything, even as I continued on my way, counting my jogging steps at that point.

A moment later – *but what is a moment when you're in a hyper state?* – I saw them both, and my world changed forever.

A dog came sprinting out of a side street a few yards ahead of me, racing towards the centre. I had no doubt that it was Willow. And it was obvious that he was chasing that man sprinting onto the bridge. That was Michael, surely. Another surge of emotion, like all my inner organs had completely crumpled, slowed me to a crawl. Anticipating a calamity, I slumped onto my knees.

Willow must also have felt something. I saw him keel over onto his flank on the pavement as if he'd been blasted by an invisible, silent force.

The man, without breaking from his sprint, leapt onto the bridge parapet and briefly looked back along the street.

Michael!

He jumped off. As soon as he was out of sight there was a monumental explosion, the flash sending a spear of pain into my eyes; the percussion like gravel in my ears. I slumped back onto my buttocks: whether as a result of the blast or simply the shock of the scene I still haven't been able to decide.

People everywhere began screaming. Galvanizing myself, and still hyperaware, I suppressed my emotions and reopened my eyes. Willow lay prostrate on the ground, unmoving. It seemed as if no-one else had noticed him: either that or they didn't care in the aftermath of the blast. Some were already leaning over the parapet, gawking, hankering for a million-view video, but the majority of people were fleeing away from the bridge, screaming with terror. Sirens wailed in the distance.

Instinctively, I knew what had happened. Michael had indeed 'vamoosed'. And, in that harrowing moment, I realised exactly what it was that I was destined to do.

I walked calmly up to Willow, stroked his head and ruffled his ears.

"Willow, your friend's gone," I said calmly. "We have to go now. Quickly!"

Without hesitation, Willow stood up and followed me. I led him back home at a quick walking pace interspersed with more trotting. Everyone was fleeing the centre so we melded in. I was keen to be nested up before the spols started cordoning off streets and asking questions of bystanders.

Bizarrely, despite the cataclysmic events of the last hour, the only thing I could think of, as Willow maintained a steady hand's span from my right ankle all the way home, was:

How do I feed a dog on a vegan diet?

♦ ♦ ♦

I felt tired. The events of the day had exhausted me physically and mentally, leaving me feeling as if my body was an empty, frail shell, devoid of energy.

Mimi had been kind to me and was now settled on the sofa. She also looked exhausted and had curled up in a semi-foetal position, snuggled up into herself, absorbed by the images on the wall. Her aura was neutral and calm, her aroma still sweet from the shower that she'd taken. This homely scene was warm and comfortable, a lullaby of emotion. I leapt up onto the sofa, burrowing my way under her arm and onto her lap, whimpering softly.

"Oh, Willow. Poor puppy."

First Jake and now Michael: it feels as if each has taken a piece of my spirit with them on their onward journey, leaving me weakened. I can't afford to lose Mimi as well or there will be nothing left.

I saw how their auras intertwined and pulsated back at the house. They were pure soulmates. She is my destiny now.

Must look after Mimi!

Must!

♦ ♦ ♦

Home was quiet after the tumult of the city. I showed Willow the small backyard which would serve for his imminent needs then showered and changed into my snuggly. It was still early but I was beginning to feel shivery as a result of the tumultuous events of the day. I sourced a suitable bowl for Willow's water – boy, was he thirsty – then tried him on some tofu. He looked at me as though I was trying to poison him. I chewed and swallowed some to show him that it was food.

"Willow, it's tasty. Go on…"

He remained unconvinced – for now. He walked away and flopped down with a whirlwind sigh. Dejected and exhausted. No wonder.

Also tired, I flopped onto the sofa, activated the wall and linked the 'Pulse. Willow soon joined me for a cuddle.

"Oh, Willow. Poor puppy."

Very comforting. I need his closeness.

"Explosion. The city. Today," I said. The wall soon filled with images of Michael and the damaged bridge, which had been closed pending structural assessment and repair. Traffic was gridlocked in the city. I changed to video. Droneyes had captured everything from the time that Michael had leapt off a bus until the explosion. I soon tired of the reporting when it switched to inane interviews with people who knew nothing about what had happened but had plenty of opinions about everything.

Reluctantly, I called for the city news channels. Michael again. Some amalgamation group was claiming him as the first white Caucasian hero to take up the Cause within his own city. A true leader, an innovator, a visionary, that's what they were calling him. More would follow in his path. The mayor called him a luckless, deluded and failed terrorist.

I realised then that the spols would come calling. I would be interrogated but I knew they could put nothing on me. I was Michael's friend from school, that's all, and I may have been starting a liaison with him. There was no more, and they would dig up no more. Willow was the one with the knowledge but he was hardly in a position to tell. So let them come, we'd see that through, Willow and I.

The casts soon changed to focus on the rally. No-one had been killed. Not other than Michael, anyway, and that was a victory as far as the city was concerned. The bluehead march had been well attended but the authorities had called off the speeches in the aftermath of the explosion. The angry thugs had broken through the spol cordons and rampaged through a district, stoning and firebombing shops and homes. Droneyes showed live footage from the riots. The spols were struggling to restore order.

Unruly, evil bastards! Someone has to put a stop to this barbaric behaviour!

EPILOGUE

CONVERGENCE

The location was perfect. Near the edge of the treeline the light intensified. Shafts of diamond iridescence appeared and vanished in time with our steps as we walked out from the womb of the forest into the dazzling, reflected brilliance of the caldera lake. The air was still, perhaps unnaturally so, as if the universe was watching us, holding its breath. The encircling slopes funnelled our view upwards towards the infinite sky, where we drank our fill and gorged on the blue.

Settling now, each of us was subsumed into the realm of that space. Our own stillness resonated with the air, the lake, the mountains, the forest. As one we breathed, deep, deep. Then, melding, our breaths meshed with the beat of the earth, and we flew, flew in tune with the dance of the universe.

♦ ♦ ♦

As night fell, we transitioned out of our meditative state, each of us resting lightly, regaining the sense of our bodies.

Our paths had been many, often intertwining. Now, as the aurora played around the moons, we embraced, pulsing with shared energy, and our spirits, converging, transfigured and joined the riders of the cosmic surf.

ABOUT THE AUTHOR

Alex Torres worked as a scientist and engineer for over twenty years in locations ranging from the Antarctic to the wilds of Lancashire. He left the rat-race in 2005 to help his wife run a boarding kennels and dog rescue operation. His love of music led him to begin writing for a number of rock music magazines and internet sites. His first book, "The Fifties Child: A Social History Through the Songs of Barclay James Harvest" was published in 2013. This is his first novel.

29188910R00164

Printed in Poland
by Amazon Fulfillment
Poland Sp. z o.o., Wrocław